BURNED PROMISES

WILLOW WINTERS

No part of this publication may be reproduced, stored in a retrieval system, or transmitted in any form or by any means, electronic, mechanical, photocopying, recording, scanning, or otherwise, without the prior written permission of the publisher, except in the case of brief quotations within critical reviews and otherwise as permitted by copyright law.

NOTE: This is a work of fiction. Names, characters, places, and incidents are a product of the author's imagination. Any resemblance to real life is purely coincidental. All characters in this story are 18 or older.

Copyright © 2016, Willow Winters Publishing. All rights reserved.

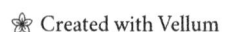

❦ Created with Vellum

INTRODUCTION

My world is caving in on itself; the scars of my past threatening to consume me.
　I was ready to fall from the top of my empire and I didn't give a damn.

But then she showed up; falling back into my life and into my bed.
　My sweetheart.

I'm not the type of man to make promises. But long ago I made one to her, and then broke it, pushing her as far away as I could. She's too good for this shit and I couldn't risk her.

I should let her walk away again; I'm a bad man, but I'm too selfish.
　This time, I'm keeping her.

PROLOGUE

Derek

It's been five years. Five long, tiring years since I've felt the gentle touch of her soft lips pressed against mine. She was such a beautiful distraction back then. A sweet girl full of innocence who I could never have. *My sweetheart.* My Emma.

I'd call her my high school sweetheart, but that's not what she was. Our relationship was a secret. Stolen kisses and private moments. We weren't supposed to be together. And we made sure to hide it.

I was tainted by my reputation, but I didn't want to be. I didn't choose this life. It chose me

I can still hear the smack of the belt. I can still feel the crunch of my jaw from when my father's fist slammed against it. At only ten years old, I was his punching bag. My Ma wouldn't let it continue though.

She took me away from him, but couldn't afford much on her own. We had nothing.

So I took the limited opportunities I had. And they led me down a path I knew better than to take.

Emma knew it, too. She knew I was bad news the second she saw me.

The good girl doesn't date the drug dealer. That's not written in any fairy tales.

I take a sip of my whiskey and relish the burn as it travels down my throat and through my chest. The glass clinks against the mantel as I set it down gently, the crackling sounds of the fireplace filling the living room.

"Derek?" There's a hesitation in Emma's voice, and I know why. I turn to take her in, those tempting curves and gorgeous hazel eyes. Her sun-kissed skin looks even more radiant from the glow of the fire.

It ended back then exactly how it should've. With her realizing I was no good, and walking away. No reasons were given, but I didn't need them. She saw enough and walked away. She had to protect herself.

It hurt; I know it hurt her too, but that's the way these things go.

"Yeah, sweetheart?" I ask as I turn to her, leaving the mantel and walking across the spacious room to set my knee on the cognac leather sofa she's lying on. She sits up as I get closer, pulling the cream chenille throw tighter around her shoulders. She's hiding herself from me; I want her naked and bared, but I'll allow it for now.

The bad boy isn't meant to have the good girl. My life was hard and dangerous; there was too much that could've happened if she'd been home in my bed while I went out and made this life for myself. I made more than a life. I carved out a reputation that creates fear, and commands respect.

I'm not just a drug dealer anymore. Now, I run this town. Every piece of it. If there's a business I don't own, you better believe they owe me in some way. I didn't ask for this, but when you have the wealth and power I do, opportunities fall in your lap. And I took them.

"I'm sorry," she says and her voice cracks and she looks away, avoiding my gaze.

It breaks my heart.

I cup her chin in my hand and lift her lips to mine, giving her a soft touch she's not used to. I'm not used to it either. The warmth of the fire hits my back in soothing waves as I pull away from her. Her eyes close, and her breath comes in shorter pants. I've never had anyone else in my life like her and now that she's back I'm not ready to give her up again.

"Nothing to be sorry about," I declare, but even as I say the words, I feel my heart squeezing in my chest with a pain that won't go away. She starts to say something else, but I'm quick to put my finger to her lips, hushing her. "It's alright, sweetheart."

I don't want to talk about what happened back then. I don't want to think about all that shit.

Life's different now. I may still be in this lifestyle, but I'm on top. And I need her now more than ever.

She didn't know why I was so eager to get lost in her touch back then, and she still doesn't know now.

I don't need a reason.

I'm ready to take what I want.

And I want her.

CHAPTER 1

Emma

I TAKE a look out of Sandra's bay window at the light dusting of snow falling. It's picturesque with the thick, crinkled, baby blue satin curtains pulled back, and a bouquet of white and red roses with baby's breath in the center sitting on the windowsill.

It's so beautiful here, back in my home town. It doesn't snow like this down south where I go to school. Sometimes I wish I'd stayed up here. Although now that my parents are getting a divorce, it's probably best I stayed away.

I sit back on my sister's cream tufted sofa, the gorgeous fireplace roaring with life. A flat-screen TV nestled between the built-in bookshelves is playing the soft sounds of some real housewife show that happened to be on when I crashed on the sofa. At least I still have my sister. My parents never really seemed to love each other anyway.

It hurts. Even though I know they'll be happier apart, I can't help but wish they'd be happy together.

Sandra saw the bitter divorce coming. She'll be happy if they never speak to each other again.

It sucks to think that way, that people who once loved each other should stay apart. I shift on my sister's couch to get comfortable and try to ignore these gloomy thoughts.

It happens, and it's for the best.

I roll my eyes, thinking about my last breakup. Breaking up with Michael was *definitely* for the best.

My heart squeezes a bit, not from missing him, but from the loss of a connection with *someone*. Some days I feel so alone, like I'm never going to have someone special in my life. I take in a deep breath and let out a heavy sigh, picking at my finger nails.

Closing my eyes, I remember how my mom told me she settled. I will *never* settle. I don't want to end up like my mother.

I cringe inwardly at my thoughts, but it's true.

I think I've settled with every relationship I've ever had, except my first.

If that even counts as a relationship.

I was scared to even whisper the word "boyfriend" around Derek. I counted each day waiting for it to end. I knew it would, it wasn't ever going to last. He was my first in a lot of ways, but I didn't give him my V-card. If I could do it all over though, I'd go back and give it all to him. I'd strip down in a heartbeat in the back of his old beat up Honda and let him claim every inch of me.

How awful is that? Maybe it's because with him, I didn't feel like I was settling. I felt whole with him. I looked forward to our private moments in the back of his car after school. Sometimes I'd sneak out at night and go to his house. I'd creep into his backyard, and tap on the window to his room. He never made me wait long.

I think he really liked it when I did that.

I think he felt the same way about me.

But that was high school, and Derek was a bad boy.

I've always been a good girl, but for him I broke the rules. For him, I did whatever he wanted, and that was dangerous. Too dangerous.

I snuggle into the sofa and sigh softly, remembering the way he held me. As if my body was meant to be held by his.

It all happened so naturally. Day one, he took me home and I wanted to kiss him, so I did.

Day two, he called me over to his table in the cafeteria to sit with him during lunch, so I did.

I walked straight to where he parked that day after school and he was waiting for me. As if we'd made plans.

We didn't have to talk about it. We didn't need a label. We just fell into place.

I roll my eyes again and readjust the book on my lap. If only it could be that easy again.

I take another look around and try not to be jealous of how freaking beautiful my sister's house is. She's now a night nurse, and obviously making bank.

I'll never make that kind of money.

I live in a cramped, but affordable, apartment, and there's no way I'll land a job making a high enough income to afford a house like this. But I'm fine with that. I want to give back and be there for the kids who need help. I'm almost there. I only have one more semester to go until I graduate.

I always knew this job was for me. Deep down, I know I can make a difference. I'm petite, and I have a young face with a higher-pitched voice, causing most people to not take me seriously. But that works to my advantage when it comes to the younger kids in the program. I've always been a people watcher, and I'm not a threat. People don't try to hide around me because there isn't a reason to. I'm not a threat. I have a gift for understanding personalities.

They try to put on a show with their bad behavior, but I see who they really are. And that's the first step to getting them help. They can open up to unsuspecting, little ole me and that makes me proud. It makes me feel fulfilled.

Right now I need to study though. I look down at the book in my lap and almost groan out loud.

These chapters on morals and ethics aren't going to read themselves. I've highlighted almost every line in the last three chapters, and I still have no idea what I've read. I just can't focus. Being home for break is throwing me off my usually good study habits.

A creak from behind me and the clicking of heels on the tile followed by the clank of keys being tossed onto the table in the hall makes me sit up straight. Oh thank God; Sandra's home. My lips kick up into a smile, a distraction!

Maybe she'll want to open a bottle of wine and watch a chick flick. I deserve a break tonight, and Sandra's always good for a girls' night. No matter where life takes us, I know that much. There's something about the bond between sisters that will always bring us back together.

As Sandra walks into the wide doorway, I start closing my books and putting my stuff back in my Kate Spade pebbled leather tote. It was a Christmas gift from her, and I freaking love it. I wanna make sure she sees I'm already using it. I make a mental note to remember to buy her something really nice for her birthday.

"Hey," she says as she drapes her tweed pea coat on the back of the sofa. She pulls her hair over her shoulders and walks straight to the fire. "It's fucking freezing out there." Her cheeks are bright red from the cold. I *hate* the cold.

"Yeah, but it looks pretty," I answer back, and she snorts a laugh. We *both* hate the cold.

"What are you studying tonight?" she asks as she casually drops onto the couch next to me.

"Morals and ethics."

"Well, that sounds fascinating!" she says sarcastically, and I grin.

"Yeah well, I'm done for the night." I lie on the sofa, putting my feet on the seat right by her thighs. "How was work?" I ask.

"Busy. I'm exhausted." She yawns as she leans back into the sofa.

"Feel like opening a bottle of wine and vegging out in front of the TV?" I stare at the ceiling, feeling like a slacker. "I can't study anymore tonight." I didn't really study at all, but she doesn't need to know that.

"Actually, Tony's on his way over," she says easily and then covers her yawn. "We were just going to hang out here for a while."

"Oh, okay. I'll get out of your way then." *Tony.* Her boy toy. I haven't met him yet, so I'm definitely going to sneak down while he's here. I don't wanna step on her toes while I'm visiting, but I'm not passing up a chance to see who she's always talking about.

"I really should be studying anyway," I say and a yawn slips out of my mouth at the last word. I blame her yawn; they're addictive.

"No!" she says, smacking my leg. "Stay and hang out with us! I really want you to meet him," she says, giving me a pleading look. "And he's bringing a friend over, so you won't be a third wheel."

I have to stop myself from groaning. She better not be trying to set me up. I have a bad feeling that's exactly what she's doing.

It's her style and the men she picks are *never* my type. I bite my tongue at that last thought. "You deserve a break," she says softly, giving me puppy eyes again. "You've been working so hard."

"Okay," I say halfheartedly. I'm not really looking forward to being set up. I put a little more pep into my voice. "Sounds good! I'll hang out for a little bit, and then get back to studying." That's a lie. I'll hang out and then go crash upstairs. Fuck studying, but it's a good excuse to bail later tonight. All this hard work has made me lame. But whatever, I need my beauty sleep. The thought forces another yawn out, as if my body agrees.

"I'm gonna go change out of my scrubs before Tony gets here." The sofa groans as Sandra gets up, pushing herself off the couch.

I follow her up the stairs, grabbing my tote and bringing it to the guest room Sandra's letting me stay in. I need to put on *real* clothes at least. I'm not meeting Tony and his friend in my PJs.

I pull baggy sweater over my tank top and pair it with some worn jeans. They'll never know I'm not wearing a bra. I chuckle softly at the thought, but the smile vanishes when I see myself in the mirror on the dresser. I look rundown. There's just no hiding the dark circles around my tired eyes. I'm exhausted. At least my hair is still decent from this morning. Not that it really matters. I'm not trying to impress either Sandra's boyfriend, or whoever his friend is.

"He's here!" Sandra calls out from somewhere downstairs. She sounds giddy and excited. It's kind of cute to see her so worked up over this guy.

The front door opens as I walk back down the stairs, my hand gripping the railing. My steps slow as I watch Tony come in. He's tall, dark, and handsome. But what's better is that he smiles when he sees Sandra.

That makes me really happy and I can't deny the smile

creeping up on my face. There's a joy reflected between the two of them that warms my heart. She squeals and runs down the hall as he kicks off his boots, dusted with snow.

"Hey, baby," he says as he wraps his arms around her waist. She holds onto his shoulders as he leans her back slightly and kisses her. I nearly roll my eyes, but that's just the jealousy in me thinking, *get a room*!

"Hey, yourself," she answers playfully. She smiles back with a blush on her cheeks, pulling away and looking at me for a split second.

I feel like such a third wheel.

"Em, I want you to meet my boyfriend, Tony." She twirls back and forth a little on her heels, still holding his hand. "Tony, this is my baby sister, Emma."

I walk down the rest of the steps and toward him with a smile.

"Hey, nice to meet you," he says as he shakes my hand. It's a firm shake, and his large hand makes mine feel small. I definitely approve.

He seems kinda familiar. It's not a small town, but maybe we went to high school together. I rack my brain, but come up with nothing.

The front door clicking shut pulls my attention away from the happy couple.

I suck in a breath and freeze in my spot. My stomach drops as I stare with wide eyes at the person standing in front of the door. My heart slows, and my body heats.

No fucking way.

Derek Wade.

"Em, this is Derek, Tony's friend," Sandra says absently. I can't respond. *Derek*. I swallow thickly, remembering how we last left. We didn't even say goodbye to each other. My heart beats slower and slower, and blood rushes into my ears. This is a fucking nightmare. I feel so awkward. I have the urge to just turn around, run upstairs and hide. But I don't want to, I never wanted to run away from him.

He's just standing there, casually shrugging his coat off his shoulders as if there's no tension, nothing there between us.

He's acting like I'm no one special, so maybe he doesn't remember me. The thought makes my throat dry and close.

For me... he was my first love. I can't deny that. Even if we were a secret.

Even if the words were never said. I wasn't brave enough to tell him, but I know what I felt for him was love.

I struggle to breathe as Derek walks closer to me.

I can feel my cheeks flaming, and I hope it's not obvious.

No one knew back then. I never told a soul. It was a secret. Even if we never called it that, we both knew what it was. We snuck around, fooled around. I almost gave him everything... I *wanted* to give him everything. I was just waiting for him to pull the trigger and make things official. But he never did.

I wish I could look away, but I can't. His pale blue eyes are piercing into me, holding me in place. They used to mesmerize me back then, but now they feel colder.

The heat between us is still there though. All of the feelings and memories from high school come pouring back into my mind. The nervousness, the excitement, the bliss when he first talked to me. Then the heartbreak, and rejection when it ended. God, I feel so naive. So young. So lost.

He's even more gorgeous now than he was back then.

He sure as fuck isn't a boy anymore. His shoulders are broader, stretching the Henley tight across his chest. His arms are so much thicker, corded with muscle. He's still tall, making me feel so small beneath him. I love it though, just as I always have. He makes me feel protected.

It's odd because he radiates a confidence and power that

would cause fear if I didn't know him. But even after all these years, I feel as if I do know him. And he doesn't scare me one bit.

"Derek, this is my sister, Emma."

"Hi, Emma," Derek says coolly. It hurts that he's just pretending he hasn't met me before. My heart does a flip, but the wrong fucking kind. The kind where it buckles and lands hard in my chest. The kind that hurts.

Whatever. I guess that's what I get for leaving him. I swallow the lump in my throat, squaring my shoulders.

Once I found out he was dealing, I just didn't want to be caught up in that. He always kept everything private. I couldn't unsee it though. Maybe it was judgmental. Maybe I was too much of a goody two-shoes. But I was falling hard for him, and I was scared that if I didn't leave at that point, then I'd never leave. *I knew better.*

My mouth is so dry. *Get a grip, Emma! He's just a guy you had a thing with in high school.* So what if he was my first kiss, stolen in the back of his car after school? So what if I felt more for him than I've ever felt before?

It's over now.

You've moved on, and he's moved on. I take a deep breath, straightening my back.

"Hi, Derek." I finally look away, not knowing how to play this.

There's only one thing I know for sure.

I'm lying to myself about moving on.

CHAPTER 2

Derek

A few moments before

I'M PISSED that Tony's so fucking insistent I get out of the house tonight. He knows I wanna be home.

I don't do the party scene. I never have. I'm not interested in mingling with clients. I've always treated this as a business. That's all it is to me, and it fucking pays me like an empire should.

That's what this is now, an empire and moneymaker. I went from a kid dealing dope, to a boss producing the best weed there is and streamlining the business.

I'm only in it for the money though, and it's getting old. I have more than enough at this point, and I don't have my heart for it like Tony does.

The cold winter wind whips across my face as Tony

BURNED PROMISES

knocks his boots against the front step of his girlfriend's place. The bitter bite of the wind makes me close my eyes and turn my head slightly. The knock, knock, knock of his boots is the only thing I can hear. We just left the last client, who's a big spender, but that didn't change a damn thing. I don't mingle. This is business only for me.

A part of me hates him for pushing me to come out, but another part is just grateful to have someone like him in my life.

He just wants me out of the house. I love him like a brother, and that's the only reason I'm here.

He's been my best friend since I could remember. We grew up next door to each other and without him, I don't know where I would be now. Probably...*definitely*... six feet under the cold, heavy dirt.

With the shit we've gotten into over the years, I know I can trust him. He's the *only* one I can trust.

He opens the front door, and I'm slow to follow him in. I don't take orders from him. I should just head home. But I don't want to. I don't want to face what's waiting for me back there. I let out a heavy sigh and kick my boots once on the step. Stalling to go in.

It makes me feel like shit just thinking that. But it's the truth.

I hear a faint female voice from inside, and I suck it up. It's just one night.

The second I'm inside, the tiny bit of hate I have for Tony grows exponentially.

Maybe he didn't know. No one really knew back then.

But my Emma, my sweetheart, is standing right fucking there. It takes me a second to really believe it. I'm frozen in place, my body tingling with recognition.

I swallow, and the sounds of everything around me seem

so fucking loud. I have to force myself to breathe and get myself together.

I hold my breath as I shut the door and act like I'm not affected.

I don't look at her, but my heart's trying to climb up my throat and get the fuck out.

Emma Fletcher.

Her sweetheart-shaped face and soft beauty have always stayed with me. She's a girl I knew I could never have back then. I hid the real me from her. I didn't let her know what I did, and the life I led. She was my secret.

She only gave me a taste and I was fine with that. When things were the hardest they'd ever been in my life, I got lost in her. I fucking loved it. I lived for those stolen moments.

Until it all went to shit.

The last time I saw her was at her high school graduation. I don't even know why I went. I graduated a year before her. I had a drop-off out front, some kids looking to party after the ceremony. But the reason I went in? I have to admit it's because I knew she'd be inside. I hadn't seen her in so long. I just wanted a glimpse of her.

I don't know if she saw me, but I sure as fuck saw her. She sat in the third row. All the way at the end. She stared straight ahead, never turned toward me, never spared me a glance.

I knew then that if I didn't say anything to her, I'd probably never see her again. She was off to college, that much I was sure of. She was always smart, and she had a future ahead of her.

And where was I going? Nowhere fast.

I wanted to talk to her. I wanted to grab her by her waist and pull her into my arms before she walked out of that door. But watching her father and mother walk up to her, her sister clapping her hands and hugging her...

It all only emphasized how different we were. How we weren't meant to be together.

I let her walk away from me that day without fighting it.

I felt regret for weeks; maybe months, I don't know. It's hard to remember with four years between now and then.

But I know for a fact I've never felt this way about anyone else. Never.

And now she's standing right in front of me.

"Em, this is Derek, Tony's friend," Tony's girlfriend says, and I finally shrug my jacket off and face Emma.

God damn it's hard to act like I'm not shaken up in the least. "Derek, this is my sister, Emma."

I can tell she's conflicted. She doesn't know what to say, or how to act. I ignore the pain in my chest.

"Hi, Emma," I push the words out.

"Hi, Derek," she says so softly, I almost don't hear her.

I have to clench my jaw at the sound of my name on her lips. She practically whispers it. The moment my name slips from those beautiful lips, she's turning and heading for another room.

My heart feels so fucking heavy. My body's tense. I immediately regret handling it that way. Fuck. There's no protocol for this shit.

"Emma!" her sister shouts after her. Sandra... That's right. I remember Sandra.

Everything starts clicking into place as I start to take off my boots and leave them on the front mat.

Sandra's my age. Same as Tony. And she's from our high school.

Fuck, I shoulda known that's who Tony was seeing. I remember her now. She didn't really run in our circles back then. She was in our grade though, and Emma's a year younger. I run my hand over my face. Damn, I wish I'd been prepared for this.

"You good, bro?" Tony asks me like this is fucking funny.

I hold in the heavy sigh of agitation and nod once. "Yeah," I answer him simply. My heart pounds faster in my chest as I say, "Let me take my boots off." He looks back at me and nods with a smirk as he follows Sandra into the room that Emma took off into.

I can barely hear them talking. The blood rushing in my ears is too fucking loud to hear clearly. But a moment later there's laughter, and I feel like I can breathe.

Between the three of them, I can make out Emma's voice the easiest. So sweet and soft, the best sound in the world, but she's nervous. I take a look back behind me at the simple white colonial door and think about just leaving.

Some part of me is screaming inwardly to get the fuck out of here. This isn't good. Not because of her, but because of me. I'm no good for her. I'm not good for anyone.

But I fucking want her. And she's never been able to tell me no.

I ignore the part of me that's desperate to keep the promise I made to myself the day she walked away. I remember it like it was yesterday.

I take in a slow and steady breath as the vision of her looking back at me over her shoulder, walking away and not saying a damn word, silently ending it with me, pops into my head. On that day I just lowered my gaze to the cafeteria table and let her walk off.

I had to grip the table to keep from getting up and chasing her down, demanding she tell me why, even though I already knew.

I promised myself that day that she deserved better, and I'd let her save herself.

But right here, right now? Fuck that.

I crack my neck and decide right then that she's mine. My feet walk of their own accord, taking steady strides into the room. I let her walk away once. But that's not gonna happen again.

I stop short when I get into the room.

Tony's already got a blunt going and is passing it to Sandra. The two of them are cuddled up on the white leather sofa on the right side of the room. My girl is across from them on the far end of the loveseat, closest to the fireplace, pretending like she's watching TV as she bites her thumbnail.

I guess she never quit that nervous habit. She looks so damn tired, like she used to look late at night when she'd beg me not to take her home. *"Just a few more minutes,"* she'd plead with me. The thought brings a soft smile to my lips. She's still fucking beautiful. Just more of a woman now.

I take a seat on the other end of the loveseat, getting as comfortable as possible and glance at the television. My brow furrows when I see it's some chick show on Bravo.

What's this shit? Is this what Tony does on his time off?

I look over at him, trying to keep the judgment off my face. I thought he was pussy whipped before, but now I know it for a fact.

I clear my throat, but I don't say anything even though I can feel Tony's eyes on me as he laughs a little. Sandra leans into him, wrapping her hands around his forearm and whispering in his ear.

I lean forward and tap Emma to get her attention, but Tony speaks up before I can say anything. "So how long are you in town?" Tony asks Emma. She looks back at me for just a split second and then at Tony and answers him, "Five weeks."

"What are you in town for?" I ask her. I can see her breath hitch, and she slowly turns to answer me.

"Just winter break... from school." Her gorgeous hazel eyes reach mine for a moment before she tucks a lock of hair behind her ear. Just hearing her voice takes me back.

I nod my head and shift in my seat a little as Sandra speaks up, her eyes already a little red from the joint she's passing between her and Tony. "Emma's in school for child psychology at Johns Hopkins."

"That's cool," I answer easily, although in my head I'm trying to think how far away that is. Fuck, that's hours away.

"I just have one semester left," Emma says softly, her voice trailing off before she clears her throat and looks away again. Is she embarrassed? I open my mouth to ask her what she's thinking, but her sister butts in.

I'm trying not to get irritated, but I just want a moment alone with Emma.

"Oh! And she has this really cool job working with kids at a local middle and high school," Sandra says with pride, but it only makes Emma blush more furiously.

"You're working with high school kids?" I ask her.

"Yeah, the bad ones," she says a little playfully, and it makes Tony laugh from across the room.

That's my sweetheart. *Loosen up for me, baby.*

I nod my head slowly as I ask, "Did you always wanna do that?" I don't know why I ask her. The question just slips out.

"She's always been super smart," Sandra says before accepting the blunt from Tony and leaning in for a kiss.

I know she has. I know my girl. It makes me proud that she's going to school for something like psychology and working with kids.

The room's quiet for a minute as I stare at her, waiting for more, but she's not giving me anything.

Emma tenses somewhat, but she doesn't move. She's waiting on me. I guess that's fair. She made the first move all those years ago.

She's gonna have to wait though. I just wanna soak her in and watch her. She needs to relax.

Tony passes me a blunt, leaning forward but not getting

his ass off the sofa. I light up, sucking in a deep breath and lean back. The flow of the smoke feels good as it fills my lungs.

Just taking that first puff, not even that, just feeling the blunt on my lips and smelling the Lemon OG Kush is already easing some of the tension. Only a bit though. I won't feel better until I can figure out what's on Emma's mind.

Sandra nudges Tony and not-so-subtly gestures at the loveseat Emma and I are seated on. The two of them are smiling, and I know right then this was definitely a setup.

I just don't know which of the two of them initiated it, and whether or not they have any idea of our past. I never told anyone. If Emma told Sandra, and she's setting us up... that's gotta be a good sign.

"We're gonna go upstairs," Sandra says a little louder than she needs to, standing up and stretching.

Tony leaves the bag of weed on the end table.

"What?" Emma asks with a hint of desperation in her voice. I chuckle at the disbelief in her voice. *They're leaving you with me, sweetheart.*

"See ya!" Sandra calls out as she practically jogs out of the room. Tony gives me a nod on his way out, looking at me for my reaction. The car keys are in his hand, but I don't reach for them. We always take my car when we meet clients, but Tony likes to drive. I don't mind it. I settle back in my seat and return his nod.

He gives me an amused look and shakes his head somewhat as he catches up to Sandra. I'll let them think whatever they want right now. I just wanna be alone with Emma. I watch as he sets the keys on the coffee table and keeps moving.

Emma perks up real fucking quick, looking at her sister with wide eyes, but she's staring at her back, 'cause Sandra's already on the move and ignoring the obvious murderous look Emma's giving her behind her back.

I take another puff and let the smoke settle in my lungs. It should be hitting me soon.

I can't take my eyes off Emma as she watches the two of them walk out, leaving her alone with me.

CHAPTER 3

Emma

I bite down on my thumbnail, a nervous habit I've always had. I can't believe Sandra left me here with *him*. My heart is racing, and I feel like I can barely breathe.

I can't look at Derek without all of the memories I have with him flooding into my mind. All of those afternoons spent talking and making out in that beat up car.

His Honda was our safe place. I'd go wherever he took me. We just wanted to get away.

Me from my parents' fighting, and him from something, although I don't know what. He never wanted to go home. He wouldn't tell me why.

I can feel his piercing gaze on me as I turn back toward the TV, barely breathing. A shiver runs through my body as I swallow thickly.

All of those study periods sitting next to each other, all of those late nights spent talking on the phone. It's all coming back to me. I close my eyes slowly, concentrating on breathing.

"You wanna hit?" he asks as the sounds of Tony and Sandra running up the stairs fade into the background.

I force myself to look at him as he takes another puff of his blunt. My mouth parts to say something, but nothing comes out. This is so fucking awkward.

"No." I breathe the word, playing with the edge of the chenille throw on the sofa. I take a deep breath and try to calm down.

"I don't smoke. Thanks though," I say shakily. I debate on saying something to break this tension. But I don't know what to say. *I'm sorry I left you all those years ago. It sucks. I loved the way I felt with you, but I was scared. Are you still a drug dealer?* Jesus, I can't say any of that. It's been five years. And he isn't bringing it up, so I'm sure as fuck not going to.

He takes another short hit and readjusts on the sofa so he's facing me.

He's so intimidating. It's not just his dark, sharp looks, it's the way he carries himself.

I can hardly stand being this close to him without making a fucking fool of myself. He makes me feel weak.

Damnit! Why did I sit on the loveseat? We're way too close. I take a deep breath to say something else. I can't stand this tension any longer, but before I can say a single word, I get a hint of his cologne.

I read somewhere that smell carries the most memory. Polo Black by Ralph Lauren, his signature scent. Just like he used to wear in high school. It's my favorite. I always think of him whenever I smell it.

I close my eyes and take another deep breath. God, he smells so fucking good. I can't believe just the smell of him is making me want him so much. I can practically feel his hands on my body. He held me like he owned me; he kissed me like he needed the air in my lungs to breathe. No one else has ever made me feel like that.

I open my eyes and take a glance at him.

"So how do you like school?" he asks. My heart's beating so fucking fast, and yet he's unaffected.

His hand rests on his jeans, and I can clearly see the outline of his hard cock. I draw in a sharp breath, looking away.

I stare down at the floor as my cheeks flame. Jesus! I'm blushing like a fucking thirteen-year-old girl. We never took it that far, but I sure as fuck wish we had. I remember grinding on top of him in the driver's seat as he kissed my neck. The sexiest sound I've ever heard was him moaning because of my touch.

"Um, school's good." I clear my throat and turn to face him a little more. "It's a lot of work, but," I force myself to look up at him and into his eyes and not back down to his dick as I continue, "I like it. And it'll be worth it in the end."

"You always did put all of your effort into school," he says, smirking. He takes another drag. "That's great, though," he adds as he exhales and blows the sweet-smelling smoke away from me. He never smoked around me back in high school. He hid a lot from me back then.

He looks sexy as fuck doing it.

I can't stop staring at his lips, remembering how soft, yet demanding they felt against mine.

"How's, uh," I pause as I have no idea what he's doing now. "What do you do?" I ask him, my forehead pinching.

He takes a long drag, and exhales slowly. I waiting, watching him as he quickly licks between his thumb and pointer finger and pinches the blunt out. Oh, the things he used to do to me with that tongue, even if we only ever made out. When he'd lick and kiss my neck, it was the most intense feeling. The subtlety and gentleness were so unexpected.

The thought makes my nipples pebble, and my breath come in short pants. It's been way too long since I've gotten laid. I've been focused on school. I can't believe I'm getting turned on watching him put a joint out.

"I'm in business now," he answers and glances up at the TV. His eyes stay focused on it even though we both know he's not watching it.

Awkward. Did I ask the wrong question?

This time he takes a deep breath, rolling the blunt between his fingers absent-mindedly as I wonder what's going on in his head.

After a minute he huffs a short chuckle and asks, "Do you remember all of those notes we used to pass back and forth?"

A small laugh sneaks out from my lips and a blush warms my cheeks. I bite my bottom lip, stifling my smile and remembering free period. "I do. And all of those doodles you'd draw." I can feel the grin grow on my face. I can't help it. "I especially liked the ones of Mr. Clinko. Remember how mad he'd get when everyone would continue to talk after he told us to quiet down?"

"And that vein in his neck would start popping out. Good times," he says, leaning back and tapping his fingers against the armrest. Him bringing that up soothes so much of the anxiety running through me. Or maybe it's just the memory.

"We did have fun." I give him a shy smile as I add, "You always distracted me from whatever I was supposed to be studying."

He nods his head slightly, the trace of a smile still on his lips, and the conversation ends there. I sit silently beside him, not wanting to bring up what happened between us, or how things ended.

I pull my legs up and sit cross-legged. I should apologize. I know I should.

Out of the corner of my eye I see him run his hands

through his thick dark hair. He used to do that when he was nervous or stressed.

He takes a deep breath and asks, "So what do you do for fun now?"

I laugh nervously. "Take a nap, or just veg out with Netflix. I'm pretty boring." *But you already know that.*

He laughs with me. "You always were a good girl. Never wanting to go out and party." Slowly, a grin spreads across his lips as he says, "Except for those couple of times at Lookout Hill."

"Well, if I remember correctly, I was coerced," I flirt back. Lookout Hill is where we first made out. Where I first felt *him*. It was the only place we had complete privacy. Where we could do whatever we wanted.

"Oh really? You seemed pretty willing," he retaliates.

"Me? No! I never did anything that would get me into trouble." I can't look him in the eyes as I say that. I know I let him get farther than anyone else did. More than a few times, I was the one pushing. He never took advantage of me though. He never pushed me to do more than I wanted. The memory makes my heart clench.

"Well, why don't we change that?" he asks with his voice low and full of lust.

Fuck, this is bad. I know this is going to end with my regretting whatever happens. I hesitate to answer.

A deep, low chuckle fills the room and pulls me out of my inner panic.

"Relax, Emma," he says as he holds out the half-smoked blunt. "I was thinking along the lines of taking a hit. Just try it. It'll help you relax."

I've never smoked before. I'll probably choke and make a fool of myself. I know all the reasons I shouldn't smoke. I have a fucking speech memorized to tell the kids who get caught with it.

I'm chewing on my bottom lip again while he stares at me with those pale blue eyes.

"Hey," he says as he leans over and tugs my bottom lip free from my teeth with his thumb. "Trust me, it'll be okay." He's so close, too fucking close. The leather sofa groans as he runs the rough pad of his thumb along my bottom lip. He's telling me it'll be okay, but he doesn't realize what this means to me.

I can't move. I can't breathe. He's staring at my lips, and I want him to kiss me. But he doesn't. Instead he moves away from me, and I instantly miss his touch.

I'd do anything to get it back.

I'm going to do bad things tonight. I can feel it. But it'll be with *him*.

And I really fucking want to. All those reasons I shouldn't smoke go right out the window.

My eyes meet his. "I've never smoked before. I don't know how to," I confess nervously.

He shrugs casually, lighting the blunt and suggests, "Just shotgun it?"

"I don't even know what that means." I pull my knees into my chest and watch as he lights the end and breathes in the blunt; the tip burns to life. "God, I'm so sheltered," I moan and bury my face in my knees. I'm so embarrassed. I sound like such a loser. I tuck my hair behind my ears and look back at him. I want him. No one can blame me for that.

Derek's always had a piece of my heart, and I'm not willing to tell him no.

"That's not a bad thing. Shot gunning's easy." He scoots closer to me, so close the smell of his cologne is stronger than the pot. "I promise. I'll take a hit and then blow it into your mouth."

My heart quickens thinking about his lips on mine again. I find myself staring at his lips. I nod my head slightly. The vision of him leaning over me with his hand on my hips makes me eager to accept.

"Okay, I'll try it," I answer quickly.

He takes a quick hit, then blows it out. I feel myself pout slightly and he laughs at me, a deep sexy sound that makes me scoot a little closer to him, so my side brushes up against his. "Ready?" he asks, cocking a brow at me.

This is stupid and not going to end well. But I want to do it so badly. I want to be bad for him.

I nod my head, not trusting my voice. I'm so nervous.

He takes a long inhale of the blunt and leans in toward me. Our lips touch ever so softly. I spear my hand through his hair and wrap the other around his neck, taking advantage, but I don't give a fuck. God, he feels so strong and warm. He feels so right. He leans into me, just like I imagined. I wish he'd push further and lay me back on the sofa. The same feelings from all those years ago flow through me as I tilt my head back, breathing in deep and holding the smoke in.

He blows the smoke from his lungs into my mouth, cupping the back of my head and leaning into me. The smoke tastes sweet in my mouth. But it's his touch that makes it all worth it. I try to suck it down and hold it. I roll onto my side and away from his embrace as I feel a cough coming on.

Fuck! The smoke burns in my lungs. *Holy fuck! It's painful! Why do people do this?*

I lie over on my side of the sofa, coughing and covering my mouth. I feel like such an idiot. As much as I'm coughing though, I can't stop smiling. I feel the blush returning to my cheeks. I cover my mouth again and sit upright, feeling foolish and naive.

The smoke hurts, but it was worth it.

"Come here," he says softly, wrapping his muscular arms

around my waist and pulling me into his lap. I'm not about to say no. He puts his lips to mine and breathes into my mouth again. I take the hit, feeling his strong hands gripping my hips to keep me in place.

This is so wrong. So bad. But I want it.

This time I don't cough as much, and I only move my head to the side when I do. He takes the chance to kiss my neck.

Fuck. Yes!

I take a moment to just breathe, feeling almost winded. I'm lightheaded from his touch or the blunt, I don't know which.

He takes another puff of the blunt, leaning away from me and then putting it out on the ashtray on the end table.

He blows out easily as I finally sit up.

"How was that?" he asks, smiling at me.

"That was great," I answer somewhat sarcastically, my voice gravelly from coughing. I scoot closer into his lap though, eager for more of his touch even though the shotgun session is over.

"I've missed you, sweetheart," he says softly as he strokes my cheek with his thumb.

I can't resist him anymore, not after hearing him call me sweetheart like he used to.

I stare at his lips, and this time I don't fight the urge. I lean into him, my hand on his thigh, and kiss him softly on the lips. I'm hesitant. Every bit of me thinks he's going to deny me, like I don't deserve him and it's all in my head. Just like all those years ago. It never felt real.

I kiss him again. I meant it to be short and sweet, but it turns into something deeper. His tongue slips between my lips, and I part them, moaning into his mouth. It's so easy to fall back into his embrace.

I wish I'd never left.

I pull away briefly to look him in the eyes. The second our eyes meet, he pulls me back into him, wrapping his arms around me and gripping the nape of my neck and my hip, kissing me fiercely.

God, this feels so right. It's like nothing's changed.

His tongue strokes my bottom lip, willing me to let him in.

And I do.

CHAPTER 4

Derek

My hands won't let go of her. I push her back down to the sofa, and she spreads her legs for me like a good girl. My dick's hard as fuck. I want her. I fucking *need* her right now.

I roughly kiss down her neck as my hands roam her body.

She writhes under me. So responsive. She's always been like that.

"You can't tell me no, can you sweetheart?" I say softly as I nip her neck and slip my hands up her sweater. She's got a tight shirt on underneath. I push my hands up her sides and she arches her back, pushing her pussy into my cock.

Even that little bit of touch makes my breathing come out harder. I gotta get these fucking clothes off and get inside her.

"Derek," she whimpers. My girl is all worked up.

This is better than any dream I ever had of her coming back to me.

She wants me even more now than she did then.

I'm quick to unbutton her jeans, kissing down her flat stomach and then lower. She lifts her hips so I can pull them off and toss them on the floor.

I look over my shoulder and wonder if I should take her upstairs. But fuck it, I don't wanna ruin this moment.

Staring down at her, I see the same look I remember so well. She's vulnerable.

I cup her pussy and lean forward. Even through the thin lace I can feel how hot and wet she is.

"Are you giving this to me tonight?" I ask softly, my lips barely touching the shell of her ear.

"Yes," she breathes eagerly. *Good girl.* I pull away from her, sitting on my heels on the sofa between her legs and trail my finger down her panties. I should have taken her back then.

I never should've let her go.

I shake off the thought along with the emotions making my chest feel so fucking tight.

I don't wanna think right now. Not about the past, or anything else.

I slowly pull down on her panties, hooking my thumbs in the sides and trailing my fingers down her thighs. She squirms and lifts her hips again. I have to lean back to pull them off her legs and let them fall to the floor with her jeans.

Her skin's smooth and soft, just like I remember.

I gently kiss her legs and inner thighs, making my way up.

"Derek," she whimpers again, covering her face. Her movements are slower and relaxed, the pot taking effect and calming her ass down. I smile into her pussy.

I don't answer her. I'm not interested in talking.

When I get to where I wanna be, I gently push on her clit with my left thumb and take a long lick of her heat.

Fuck, my dick can't take much more. She's so fucking wet. So *sweet.*

I lick up her arousal, loving her taste. It's been so long. Too long. My dick's so fucking hard and aching to be inside of her.

"How much do you want me?" I ask her before taking another long, languid lick from her entrance to her clit. I flick her clit with my tongue and then suck on her. Her back bows and she tries to get away. I fucking love it.

She moans her pleasure a mix of wanting more and fighting to get away from me, her thighs trembling and her legs closing out of instinct. I have to push my hand against her inner thigh and keep her open for me. I stare up at her, holding her heated gaze as I lick her clit nice and slow.

"Derek," she moans reverently.

I latch onto her clit and push two thick fingers into her tight pussy. She's so wet, so hot. So fucking ready.

My dick twitches and pushes against my zipper.

I'll get her off first, but then I'm taking her. I resisted back then. She was too good for me, but I fucking want her right now, and there's nothing that's gonna stop me.

"Sweetheart?" I try to get her attention but she only hums slightly, her body going still. "Emma," I call out to her a little louder, pulling away from her.

She doesn't respond.

I sit up on the sofa and finally get a good look at her.

Fucking hell.

She passed out on me.

Fuck! Fucking pot has her knocked out.

"Emma!" I shake her gently, but she's not moving. And she's not gonna either; this stuff is good dope.

I run my hand over my face, wishing this wasn't fucking happening.

Finally, I look back down at her sleeping peacefully, and I give up.

I wrap her up in the throw and grab her jeans and underwear. She's so light in my arms as I take her upstairs. It's not hard to find her room. The door's open.

I lay her on the bed, and she doesn't move an inch. The only sign of life is her steady breathing.

She must've been exhausted. She's not wearing her underwear, and I don't like that. I don't want her thinking anything happened. Her legs are way fucking heavier with her not helping me, but I pull on her lacy underwear and then nestle the covers around her.

I wish I could get into bed with her.

But this is her sister's house, and I'm not staying here with the hopes of getting a morning lay.

I take one last look at my sweetheart before heading out.

THE SOUND of the driver's side door shutting to my Porsche disrupts the peaceful quiet of the night. I hit the clicker, filling the cold air with a quiet *beep beep* as I walk into my house. It's late. I left Sandra's house about thirty minutes ago and took a slow ride home, not in any rush to get back.

I'm still processing everything that happened. It's like a dream.

I touch my fingers to my lips and I can still faintly taste her. *My sweetheart.* I can't let her go this time.

I can't fucking believe she passed out on me. I shoulda known she'd be a lightweight.

But damn she felt good to hold. The smell and feel of her. *The taste.*

My dick starts hardening again, and I have to force the images out of my head. I'm not fucking jerking off. The next time I cum it's gonna be inside her. She's mine. Just like she's always been.

I know she's going to play hard to get, but nowadays I get

what I want. She can try to run, but it's not going to work this time.

A chuckle rises up my chest as I walk to the door feeling more life in me than I have in years, remembering how we first met.

I'd just started my car and was warming it up on a snowy day when I saw her leaving school. It wasn't the first time I'd seen her. I knew she was younger than me. She was gorgeous, such a sweet, shy girl with an innocence about her that drew me to her.

Her brunette hair was whipping in her face as she walked out into the snow off the worn path on the sidewalk and across the street. I watched her out of curiosity. I remember how her cheeks were so red from the cold, and her nose, too. But she looked so fucking beautiful with that baggy sweater she always wore.

I wanted more. As a kid, I never dared to want anything. But I craved her touch, even just a glance from her.

She hustled across the street and didn't even see the black ice until it was too late. I was out of my car just as she landed hard on the ice, her palms slamming against the cold hard ground. Fuck, it hurt just watching. What was worse was that the bottom of her bag split from the impact, and her books were falling out. They weren't scattered or ruined, but still. She needed help.

She sat wincing and sucking in a breath between her clenched teeth in the middle of the street. Her jeans were torn, and there was a bad scratch on her one hand.

I felt for her. I wish I could've stopped her from falling in the first place, but at least I could help her up.

I didn't speak as I bent down to help her up off her ass. Picking her up like she was mine, like I was meant to be there for her.

I'll never forget the look in her eyes. How the sight of

me took the breath from her and all of her pain seemed to wash away. There was a spark between us. I know I'm not making that shit up in my memory, 'cause it's stayed with me all these years. A heat burned between us as we locked eyes.

She seemed surprised that I even talked to her. I never talked much. Still don't. I know I was unapproachable at the time. Ma had just been diagnosed a few months back. I didn't feel like talking to anyone. I was just doing what I had to do. I was surviving day-to-day. A kid shouldn't grow up like that. It wasn't Ma's fault and I didn't blame her or anyone else. She never stopped trying.

The trace of a smile from the memory of my sweetheart vanishes from my face as I punch in the code and open the door.

Even though Ma's home, I keep it locked. She's probably sleeping anyway. The thought brings me down from the anxious high I've been riding on.

It brings me back to reality.

I close the door softly and wait for the faint beep of the security system as I slip off my boots. Bits of ice and snow fall off onto the mat as I set them off to the side and look down the hallway. Ma's on the first floor, and the light is shining through from beneath the door to her bedroom. She moved into my house a few months ago. With the cancer wearing on her, she couldn't be alone. I needed to keep an eye on her.

It's late for her to be up. And lately she's been more and more exhausted.

It's why she's down here now. She'd get so winded from climbing the stairs.

I think about just going up the stairs and crashing, but I can't.

I walk quietly to her room and knock gently, rapping my

knuckles on the door and waiting with my ear almost pressed against it.

"Come on in," I hear her say, barely loud enough to hear.

The door opens with a faint creak and she tells me, "Leave it open."

If there's anyone in this world that I take orders from, it's Ma.

I do as she says, watching the lines on the screen of the monitors as I walk closer to her. If the sound was on, there'd be a steady beep filling the room.

They're calling this hospice, which I can't stand. It's not the first time they've hooked her up for a day or two to monitor her. But I hate it when they call it hospice. She's making it through this one. Just like the last time. She's gonna be alright.

I know she is.

She's not doing too well, but she's still smiling. She's never stopped. *Smile today without fear of tomorrow.* That's her motto.

"Tell me something new, Derek," she says as I rub the sleep away from my eyes. I need to get some rest, at this point I'm working on a couple hours at most from last night. And tomorrow I have a long day, too.

For a moment I consider telling her about Emma. She's the only thing that *new* comes to mind. The only thing that matters. But as I pull the chair up closer to her bed and take my usual seat, I clear my throat and shrug. I don't know what I'd tell her about Emma anyway.

"Same ol, same ol." I answer her and sit back in my seat. My muscles ache as they try to relax against the hard back of the chair. She's got her reading glasses on and an old romance novel with worn pages closed on her lap, although her finger's holding her place.

"Did I interrupt your reading?"

Her thin lips pull into a soft smile. "Never, baby. I've always got time for you."

"You find a wife yet?" she asks, slipping the glasses off her face and tapping them against the book impatiently. "You know you're not getting any younger?"

A rough chuckle vibrates up my chest.

"There's no woman on this earth who could replace you, Ma." She rolls her eyes at the hint of sarcasm in my voice.

She puts her glasses back on, but then takes them back off and pinches the bridge of her nose.

"You alright?" I ask her, leaning forward and placing my hand gently on her elbow to steady her.

"Just a headache." Her voice is small and scratchy.

"Did you get any sleep?" I ask her. She needs it. She can't go on without resting.

"Yeah, some." She looks at me for a long moment before saying, "I'd like to see you happy before I die." Ma's words stop me short of moving, the breath stilling in my lungs.

I hate how she talks like that. As if she's leaving me tonight. She's been beating the odds for years now. The cancer was supposed to kill her years ago. She's not dying. I won't let it happen.

Ma says that prayers work wonders. I know the drugs are helping. Or at least they were. Lately, though, her skin seems a little more grey, her face a little thinner, and her energy is nowhere near what it used to be. I wanna believe it's just old age. But the scans are showing that it's spreading again.

The chemo helped, before, but this time, not so much. It just needs time. It's gonna work. I know it will. It has to.

"I mean it, Derek." Her voice is hard as she settles back against the bed and takes in a deep breath. "You gotta find someone to make you happy." My mother's eyes water as she looks at me.

"Ma, knock it off. I'm gonna be fine." Her small hand feels

so frail in mine, but she squeezes back with the strength I know she has, the strength I'm used to.

She wipes away the tears under her eyes with her other hand.

"Stop talking like that." I try to think of something the doctor said on the last visit, but there wasn't anything that I can remind her of to keep her focused on fighting this. It's quiet for a long time, neither of us knowing what to say.

I try not to let it get to me. She's gonna be fine.

"Go ahead and turn that light out for me, would ya?" she asks as she puts both the book and her glasses onto the nightstand. "I think I'll try to get in a little more shuteye."

"Alright," I say and get up, pushing off on my thighs and readying to go pass out myself. The thought of my sweetheart knocked out on the sofa makes a soft smile form on my lips.

"Love you, Ma," I tell her out of habit before I flick the switch.

"Love you, too," she says softly. "Leave it open," she tells me with my hand on the doorknob.

As I climb the stairs, I cover my mouth with a yawn and think about Emma.

I remember that day again. The day that she fell, and her bag tore. There was a goodness about her I knew I didn't deserve.

I still don't, but I want her.

CHAPTER 5

Emma

Sunlight pours through the sheer white curtains.

I open my eyes slowly, and it takes me a minute to figure out where I am. *Sandra's guest room.* That's right. *Winter break.*

It comes back to me as I rub my eyes and lie back into the soft pillow, just wanting the annoying light to go away. My head hurts and I feel like I either overslept, or didn't sleep enough. The last thing I remember is being on the loveseat with Derek.

Shit! I practically jump up, pushing the hair out of my face and frantically looking around the room.

Throwing off the lavender-colored down comforter, I climb out of bed. My head spins at first, and I brace myself against the dresser.

Oh my God.

I'm still in the black cami and lace undies I was in last

night. Just undies... I take a moment to make sure I didn't do anything stupid last night. Recalling everything I can.

Well... shit smoking was stupid. Being with Derek ... that's not smart. I cringe as I recall everything that happened last night. Covering my face with my hands.

We didn't have sex though. I know he wouldn't do that. And I don't feel like I did.

I cover my face with my hands, remembering how he was going down on me. And then I passed the fuck out. Oh my fucking God.

I was trying to tell him. It was so hard to keep my eyes open.

But it felt so good.

I groan into my hands and then crouch on the floor, leaning my back against the wall and huddling into a pathetic ball.

I cannot believe I did that. I'm so embarrassed.

I look back at my dresser and find my neatly folded jeans.

If it'd been someone else... I shake my head. I never would've done that with someone else. Never.

It was all because it was Derek. And he's different.

In school, they all said he was bad. One teacher specifically told me to stay away. Mrs. Hepburn. She was a bitch who needed to mind her own business. I feel the anger rise up all over again. They had no right to judge.

He wasn't a *bad* guy, not really. I knew he wasn't back then. He may have done some bad things, but he had a goodness about him, hidden under the hard facade. Now he's grown up, and the mask he wears is good at covering it, scaring people off, but that goodness still there.

I hear faint sounds of dishes and chatter coming from downstairs, and that's when I realize he may still be here.

I shoot up and bound through the room, digging through my worn-out black duffel bag to find my pajama pants and quickly pull them on. I practically run down the stairs, but when I look up and see his jacket is missing from the coat rack, my heart drops and my steps slow. My bare feet pad on the wooden floor, and my stomach growls as I walk towards the kitchen.

I wish he was still here so we could talk about what happened last night. We need to talk about it.

At least I do.

But maybe he doesn't. Maybe last night didn't mean much to him at all. I cross my arms and try not to think like that.

As I start making my way to the kitchen, I hear Sandra giggling, followed by Tony's voice.

She's frying eggs on the stove, while Tony stands next to her scratching his ass. "You're so gross!" Sandra says, laughing. Tony slaps her ass, resulting in even more giggling. At least Sandra seems happy. She deserves to be. I've never seen her like this, bubbly and at ease with a guy.

"Good morning," I say hoping it's not awkward that I'm interrupting them and opening the cabinet to pull out a box of Corn Pops. It's my favorite cereal. Sandra always stocks up on it when I come to visit.

"Good morning," Sandra says as Tony kisses her neck and thankfully backs away to take a seat at the small table.

"Morning," he says, stretching his back with his arms over his head. You'd think he lived here, too. Shit, maybe he does. Maybe this last week she's kept him away to give me space.

I close the cabinet and try not to think about it as I chew on the inside of my cheek.

"Is Derek here?" Sandra asks me with a ridiculous Cheshire grin on her face. She's way too excited this morning.

"No, he left last night," I tell her, ignoring the urge to try to pick apart everything that happened and over analyze why I'm here alone this morning. It's simple. He didn't want to stay, so he didn't. That's all it means. Or at least that's what I tell myself over and over again as I put the milk away and sit down at the table.

Tony sits down across from me with the fried eggs and toast Sandra just made him.

"Oh, so he didn't stay with you?" she asks turning to face me with a look of confusion.

I shake my head no, shoving the spoon in my mouth and eating a bite of cereal. "Why are you asking?" I ask stirring the pops with my spoon.

She shrugs before turning back to her omelet on the stove.

I shake my head and take another mouthful of my cereal. The room is mostly quiet except for the clinking of the spoon against the ceramic bowl, the sounds of the eggs cooking on the stove, and the gentle scraping of the spatula. Tony's on his phone, and I keep staring at him.

He knows Derek....I shove another spoonful into my mouth to keep from prying, but I can't help myself once he's off the phone.

"So, Tony, you're good friends with Derek?" I ask.

"Yeah, we've been friends for a real long time." he sets his phone down to give me his full attention. "We grew up next door to each other. I was always over his house," he answers me.

"Oh, really?" I didn't know he grew up with Derek. My skin tingles with anxiety. I wonder if he knows about us. I never saw him back then. I never saw anyone. More than a few times I went to Derek's house, but I was quiet and discreet. I always waited in the back, just like he told me to.

Neither of us wanted anyone to know.

I bite the inside of my cheek rather than snooping anymore. I need his number though. Or something. I need to get ahold of him, but asking his friend when Derek could've left it for me just seems desperate. Sandra sits down next to me with her egg whites and three strips of bacon. It smells too good. I snag one of the three pieces, and she playfully acts like she's going to stab me with her fork.

Tony takes the opportunity to grab a piece for himself while she's distracted with me, and I practically snort when she sees. Her mouth drops open in shock. Like he truly betrayed her for stealing a strip of bacon.

I lick my fingers as she takes her last and only piece and mutters, "Vultures."

Tony hands her back half of his stolen strip, and she snags it like he's gonna rip it away from her if she doesn't take it right then.

I have to admit, they're so stinking cute together.

Wanting to know more about the guy that's making my sister so happy, I ask Tony, "What do you do for a living?"

"I work with Derek," he says easily.

"What does he do?" I ask him, mostly because Derek's answer was so short and vague last night.

"He has a business. A bunch of 'em. He kinda runs the town."

He runs the town? What the fuck does that mean? I wait for Tony to say more, but he just continues eating his breakfast.

My skin tingles with anxiety. He can't still be dealing drugs. Derek was so much smarter than that. The thought makes my stomach flip.

I stir the cereal around in my bowl of milk. I don't have much of an appetite anymore. I push the bowl away and try to calm down. *Runs the town.* What's there to run? I gather my hair and pull it over my shoulder. All I can think is that he's doing shady shit. It makes me feel sick to my stomach. I want to question Tony. I want straight answers, but at the same time, I just don't want to know. Knowing I'd rather hide from the truth than deal with whatever it is that he's doing makes me cringe. I'm like one of those mothers I hate, enablers. Women who turn a blind eye while their children go further and further down the wrong path. I feel sick just thinking about it.

I drag one of my books that was on the edge of the table closer to me and flip it open. The letters seem to blend together as I read them. All the black and white print is mixing and turning grey. I blink a few times and flip the page. *Just one more semester.*

I look up at the sounds of running water and dishes being stacked together.

Tony and Sandra are washing the dishes together in the large porcelain farmhouse sink. I'm rereading the last paragraph I just read. I can't concentrate.

I can't think about anything except Derek. My phone rings and I look at the number, but I have no idea who it is. The caller ID just displays numbers on the screen. I debate on not answering, but then it hits me. *It could be him.*

"Hello?" I answer as calmly as possible, trying not to seem like I'm dying inside for it to be Derek.

"Morning, sweetheart." A wave of relief and something else go through my body when I hear his voice. "What are you up to?" he asks.

I can't help the smile on my face as I tap a pen on my textbook. I've always been so conflicted when it comes to Derek. I can't help that I want him. I'm drawn to him, even knowing it's wrong.

My face flushes as I realize Tony and Sandra are watching me closely.

"Uhh, nothing. Just studying," I say quietly, turning away from my audience. "How about you?"

I can hear Sandra whispering something not-so-quietly to Tony. I close my eyes and just ignore them.

"Not much." He's gonna ask me out. I can feel it. My eyes pop open as I wait to hear the words. God, I feel so young and naive again. "I was just thinking about you, and I need to see you again. You wanna go out tomorrow night?" he asks. *Yes!*

I start to answer how I would have all those years ago. *Of course. Whatever you want.* I would have followed him anywhere back then.

But this time, I hesitate. We were two dumb kids in puppy love. Now we're adults, and this is real life.

And I need to know what his *business* is. I tap the pen a little faster on the textbook.

"You there?" I hear him ask.

"Yeah, yeah. I'm free." I can go. I should go, if for no other reason than just to talk. But I know there's more to it than talking. I know I'm heading down a path that's going to suck me in and threaten to take over.

"*Yes!*" I hear Sandra squeal in the kitchen, her feet padding against the floor. I don't have to turn around to know she's practically running in place.

I shake my head, my hand over my eyes. I love my sister, but what was she thinking? My heart squeezes in my chest.

"Great. I'll pick you up at eight," he says in that deep voice that makes me want his lips on me.

"See you then," I say softly into the phone, feeling a mixture of emotions running through my blood.

"Bye sweetheart," he says.

I really should have said no, but the butterflies in my stomach and everything in our past are clouding my judgment.

I just hope this isn't a huge mistake.

CHAPTER 6

Derek

I've got it bad. All I wanted to do yesterday was pick her up. I knew she'd be home alone and studying. Some things never change.

I take a look at her in the passenger seat as I slow down at the red light, my Porsche humming smoothly.

She's playing with the hem of her dress and mouthing along to the song on the radio.

"I like this one," she says sweetly when she sees I'm looking at her. A beautiful blush rises to her cheeks and she tucks a strand of her hair that's escaped from her bun behind her ear.

"Why are you so nervous today?" I ask her. The way she's looking away from me and shifting in her seat makes it more than obvious that she's apprehensive about something. It's more than that though. She seems uncomfortable. Like she's second-guessing this.

There's a tension between us. I expected it. We're still

feeling each other out, I guess. We haven't talked about anything, but I don't really plan on it. I want her, so I'm taking her. It's that simple.

I don't like that she's so uneasy though. It takes her a moment before she's able to answer me. "Do you still deal?"

I hate her question. Do I still deal? Some. I'm not the dealer though. I'm the supplier. And it's pot, for fuck's sake. I look out of the window, regretting the awkward tension between us and then drive through the intersection, the quiet air becoming thick.

I lick my lips and pull into the parking lot of Mariani's Bistro. It's one of my places of business. It's close to my place, and it's a nice restaurant which should impress her.

She clears her throat uncomfortably and barely gets out, "Sorry. I shouldn't ask."

No, she shouldn't. The fewer questions, the better. There's no reason for her to know anything other than I'll provide for her. I'll keep her safe.

But she doesn't really know either of those things. She's gotta realize I'm well off by now. The suits and car shoulda given that away. Maybe that's why she's asking.

"I just heard-" she starts to say, but then she shuts her mouth.

"What's that, Sweetheart?"

"I heard you run the town?"

It's a fucking stupid expression. I don't agree with it either. I've got money and I like investing, so I've got my hands in plenty of pockets. Tony likes that particular saying though.

"Fucking Tony," I mutter, staring away from her and out the driver's side window.

"Look, last night-"

"Last night was everything I've wanted since you left me."

I can hear her looking for any excuse to bail. I see it in her eyes. But I'm not going to let her walk away so easily this time. It's not happening.

"You don't like that I deal, do you?" I'm blunt. I'll get straight to the point and put this shit to bed.

"No, I don't."

"Is that the only thing?" I ask her.

She takes in a steady breath and nods her head. It fucking sucks, 'cause it's not like this is a job I can just walk away from.

"It pays the bills. It's not really illegal."

"It is really illegal," she says straight faced.

Selling pot isn't so bad. It's legal in some states. This is a college town, and I keep my business as clean as possible. But some of the shit I've done has definitely crossed the line. I rub the back of my neck sighing before turning back to her. Just let it be sweetheart. I'll take care of her; that's what matters.

The look on her face tells me it's not going to be that easy though.

I shrug. She has no right to judge me. She doesn't know what a shit hand I've been dealt. I turn the car off and the radio dies, leaving the car filled with silence.

"I don't lose any sleep over it." That's a lie. The second I say it, I regret it. She crosses her arms over her chest, gripping onto her forearms and looking out of the window. It's dark and cold outside. Her head falls against the window gently, and her breath fogs up the glass.

She's completely closed off now, and I know it's 'cause I was short with her.

"I'm sorry, sweetheart." I never say sorry, but seeing her hurt and disappointed fucking kills me. Anyone else? I'd say fuck 'em. But it's Emma. "I just don't want you to get involved with this. You don't need to know this shit."

"But I want to be involved with you," she says so quietly I almost don't hear. "I remember how I fell for you, Derek. It's scaring me. I don't want to fall for someone who's..." she doesn't finish that sentence and it fucking shreds me.

Who's a criminal.

Who's no good for her.

"I'm not a knight in shining armor, Emma. But I'm not gonna hurt you. And I won't let anyone else hurt you either." I can promise her that. She looks away, and is quiet for a moment. The chill of the night starts creeping into the car, but I'm not starting it again. I'm taking her out, whether she likes it or not.

"Have you ever killed anyone?" Emma asks softly. Like she's afraid of the answer. She turns her head to the side, peeking at me from the corner of her eye.

I don't answer her. I don't want to. When she knew me, I was just a peddler. I needed money for Ma, and I did shit I wasn't proud of. When Emma left me, I only got deeper and deeper into this life. I had nothing else going for me.

And in this line of business, death happens.

When you have a name that people recognize, some pricks are going to challenge you. It doesn't happen anymore, but it did in the past.

The only name coming to mind right now is my father's though.

I turn away from her and lean back in my seat, running my hand through my hair. "You know you don't wanna know the answer to that, sweetheart." I can't look at her when I answer. I know just the way her forehead pinches and her beautiful lips turn down when she's upset. And I can't fucking stand it.

Killing my father didn't feel the same as the other fuckers. Those assholes had it coming. It was me or them, and it was all business, nothing personal.

When my father came back and started thinking he had rights to the money I was giving Ma, it was personal.

She needed that money. She deserves a good life, and she still doesn't know what I do. That fucker thought he could come back and beat on the two of us just like he used to. He only got two swings in until he was on the ground, choking on his own blood as I landed my fist over and over.

Tony had to pry me off of him. I don't know how long he'd been dead.

"Don't ask questions you don't wanna know the answers to," I finally tell her. I look deep into those beautiful hazel eyes and I see something I've never seen before, a hint of fear.

"I never enjoyed it. I don't go looking for trouble. But for a while, trouble came to me."

"You didn't have to-"

"You don't know, Emma." My words come out sharp, and she looks as if I've slapped her. I'm gutted by the expression on her face and the fear in her eyes.

Fuck, I wish I could pull her into my lap right now and comfort her like I used to do. I'd just hold her, leaning my seat all the way back and letting her lie on top of me. We'd make out, and she'd let me feel her up. My hands would travel along her curves, making her shiver.

I reach down to hit the button and push my seat back, so we can do just that. I'll make her forget. I'll make her not care about anything other than wanting my touch, but she speaks up, finally breaking the silence.

"I wanna be with you," she says softly, catching me off guard. "But it doesn't feel right, knowing what you do." There's so much pain in her voice.

I reach over and rest my hand on her thigh, tilting my head so I can see her.

"You aren't supposed to know," I tell her easily. "You think your sister knows what Tony does?" I ask her. I speak before thinking. I shouldn't say shit about Tony and his job. He's my enforcer. If Emma thinks it's wrong that I've killed a few men, she'd be horrified by the shit Tony's done. "He's in the *business*."

"I'm not getting into that. It's her concern, not mine" Emma says with a hard edge. I didn't expect that from her. And I don't like it.

"You knew what I did before you got in this car, Emma." I look straight ahead. Across the barrier is a parking lot to another shopping strip. It's mostly empty since it's so late, and all the stores are closed. "I can promise you, it'll never come back to you." I can say that in good faith. She's safe with me.

Emma starts biting on her thumbnail, looking out of the window and thinking. I can practically see the wheels turning in her head. She's so different from any other woman I've met.

Usually, it's the lifestyle they want. That's what attracts them to me. And precisely why I'm not interested.

She's too good for me. I've always known that. I grip the leather steering wheel and clear my throat to get her attention.

"I have other businesses, too." I have seventeen, to be exact. And the only one that has me crossing over into the grey areas of the law is the dope.

"You do?" Emma asks.

"Yeah, like this restaurant." I nod to my left.

"You own this place?" she asks as she leans forward and looks out of the window. The warm yellow glow from the large bay windows out front spills onto the pure white snow falling around the building.

"Only fifty-one percent. But yeah, it's mine. I own a few of 'em." Her sassy little mouth parts open slightly, and then closes shut. "Now you're impressed?" I ask her with a cocked brow.

She looks down at her hands in her lap and then back up at me. "Can you really blame me?" She's smiling a little, which is a good sign. At least the shock is taking away from all that other shit.

I huff a laugh at her disbelief and then shift in my seat to face her. "I'm not a bad guy. And I don't do stupid shit."

She starts to say something at that last line, and I have to cut her off.

"Not when I can help it." She looks at me warily and then settles down.

"I wanna be good for you though, Emma. I always have."

"I don't know." She swallows thickly, and I can tell she's so close to letting it go.

Don't tell me no, sweetheart. Just give in.

"Come on in with me," I tell her, taking her small hand in mine. She lets me bring her hand to my lips, and I kiss her knuckles. That gets me a small smile at least. "I just wanna feed you."

Emma laughs gently, shaking her head and leaning the back of her head against the window but staring at me. "Don't lie to me, Derek," she says playfully.

"Me? I'd never lie to you." My heart stutters in my chest. I'd keep the truth from her. That's for damn sure. But I'll never lie to her outright.

"You don't just wanna feed me," she says softly, biting her bottom lip.

"Oh yeah," I say and lean forward, resting my hand on her thigh while still holding her other hand. My thumb rubs soothing circles on her wrist. "And what is it I wanna do to you then?" I ask her. I lean closer to her, daring her to say something. My lips are only an inch away from hers.

"You wanna fuck me," she says in a breathy voice.

My cock hardens instantly. She's right about that.

"Well, I wanna feed you first." She smiles softly and then quickly gives me a peck before opening the door and sliding out, leaving me hard as fuck and wanting more.

CHAPTER 7

Emma

I'll give him just one chance. It's only one night. I can handle this.

As I climb out of the car, I pull my coat tighter around me. It's so cold. He shuts the door behind me, still holding my hand and pulling me close to him.

He wraps his arm around my waist, and I lean into him. I can feel his warmth through my jacket.

I'm so fucked. Nothing he admits will ward me away. I already know it. Even as I asked him if he'd ever killed before, I was already making excuses for him. My heart stopped beating, and my body felt cold. I wanted him to deny it, even though I already knew the truth.

I was ruined the day he took me home five years ago. That day changed me forever. I've never stopped wanting him, even knowing the person he truly is.

"So this is your place?" I ask him in a whisper as we walk up the snow-dusted path.

"I only own fifty-one percent, and I don't really do the work. I'm more of a financial investor," he answers as he opens the door. I'm instantly hit with a wave of warmth, the faint sounds of chatter surrounding us as the door closes and we're finally inside.

His restaurant is beautiful. I've never been here before, and it's definitely new. I love carbs and every Italian dish I've ever met. I want to ask him how this all happened, when it was built. But I don't want to question him if it means prying into…the *other* business. I grip my wristlet and gently clear my throat, taking in the luxurious atmosphere.

The deep mahogany floors and matching trim contrast with the cream-colored walls. Round café style tables fill the center of the room that's bordered by booths. The tables are all covered with deep red linen tablecloths, with a candle and one white rose in the center of each. Ornate wrought iron chandeliers hang from the exposed beam ceiling.

It looks so much bigger inside than it did from the outside.

He nods at the maître d', who obviously recognizes Derek, and then continues to lead me back, not stopping for a moment. His hand is splayed on my lower back as he walks us to a corner booth in the rear of the restaurant, away from everyone else.

I'm trying to calm down, but it suddenly hits me that this is more intimate, more serious than anything we've ever done.

This is a date. Like a real live date. My skin pricks, and anxiety flows through my blood as if just realizing what this is.

A public date. Not a secret. My heart beats a little faster as

I peek up at him from the corner of my eye, a violent blush lighting my cheeks on fire.

Derek Wade is...taking me on a first date. My heart flips, and I nervously tuck a bit of hair behind my ear, turning away from him.

"It's quiet back here," I say timidly as he slides into the middle of the curved booth, facing the crowd. I sit down at the end of the black leather bench, but he motions for me to sit next to him, not across from him.

"I won't bite."

Somehow my cheeks flame even hotter, and I do as he says. I slide around the circular table, and he pulls me in close. I stare at my hands in my lap, my fingers twisting around each other. I just need to calm down.

Soft classical music spills from the speakers above us and being so far in the back, it's slightly darker here, cozier.

He only wants to feed me.

The thought makes me roll my eyes, but at least it puts me at ease.

"I like the privacy," Derek says, breaking the silence. I don't have a moment to respond.

"Good evening Mr. Wade, my name is Peter and I'll be your waiter for the evening," a young man says as he approaches the table. He gives me a small, polite smile as he places a bread basket in front of us before turning his attention to Derek.

The waiter has a bit of an accent, and it takes me a moment to realize he called Derek, "Mr. Wade." He can't be any older than twenty. I'd be shocked if he is. He pulls out his pad and a pen to take our orders. His stubble is spotty. He's definitely still just a kid.

"Could you bring us a bottle of Montoya Cabernet? Scampi for our appetizer, but don't wait on our entrees to bring it out. And we'll split the penne and the risotto." Derek looks across the table at me, handing the menus on the table to the young waiter. "You're gonna love it." He smiles a sweet, reassuring grin as he adds, "Trust me."

God help me, I do trust him.

"Of course, Mr. Wade. I'll be right back with your wine," Peter says as he bows his head and turns toward the kitchen.

I finally look up at Derek, and I'm shaken up by how at ease he seems. I still can't get over the fact that he owns this place. That he took me here. I didn't expect this. Ever. No man has ever held a candle to Derek, but I hadn't ever pictured him back in my life. Now I don't know how to handle this.

If only he'd stop being a dumbass and quit dealing. I grab my white cloth napkin and shake it out, laying it on my lap. It pisses me off.

I don't understand why he'd settle on something like dealing when he has legitimate businesses like this. I wish he'd just stop. I would cave to him the moment he did. I'd be his in a fucking heartbeat.

"Tell me why," I say once the waiter is out of earshot.

"Why what?" he asks, grabbing a small slice of bread from the basket the waiter left on the table. He rips it off rather than cutting it all the way through.

Before I can answer him, Peter returns with our wine, setting the wine glasses down gently and pouring the dark red liquid into the glasses easily. Derek has him pour some wine in each of our glasses, the rich aroma filling the private space between us.

"Your meals will be out shortly, sir," Peter says before heading back down the row of tables.

I turn to face Derek with my shoulders squared. My knee hits his by accident, but that gets his attention. "Tell me why you do it."

He puts his glass down after taking a long sip, and sighs,

looking away from me. I can tell he's not happy I'm asking, but I need to know. His brow is pinched, and he taps his knuckles on the table a few times before looking back at me.

"Emma, you need to stop," he says forcefully. The stern look he gives me would have scared me if it were anyone else. I'm not going to give up though. He should know me better than that.

"Just answer me first, please. I need to understand," I plead softly. I hold his piercing gaze, ignoring the chill in his eyes.

He sighs again, tossing his white cloth napkin on the table in front of him and setting his elbows on the table. He steeples his fingers and leans his forehead against them. My heart thuds in my chest. I don't want to lose him. I don't. But I can't say yes.

Finally, he looks at me. "I don't know what you want me to tell you, Emma. I made a choice when I was a kid." He leans back, his lips set in a firm line. "I got involved with men who held it over me. They threatened me, so I stayed in line," he answers, exasperated.

"D-do they still?" I ask, afraid to hear the answer. My blood heats with anxiety.

"They're dead." His words are soft, but they fall hard. "Where they belong," he adds and waits for my reaction. His eyes have never looked so cold. So empty. Devoid of the other side of him that I know so well.

My body turns to ice as it did in the car. It scares the shit out of me.

Before I can find my voice to respond to him, he adds quietly, "I'm not in that business anymore."

That business? What is *that* business? I grit my teeth. I fucking hate these secrets. I don't like not knowing and turning a blind eye. "What do you mean?" I ask uncertainly. I feel meek. Only because I don't know what he's talking about, and I'm on the cusp of letting myself fall for a man who has another life I know nothing about. A life I don't want to be a part of.

Seeing the anxiety clearly present on my face, Derek answers, "Sweetheart, please stop asking questions. I'll tell you everything you need to know."

He reaches out and takes my hand, but the second he does the scampi comes, interrupting us and keeping his touch from calming me.

Need to know. I repeat the words in my head as the waiter sets the plate on the table.

It smells delicious, with lots of butter, and I'm starving; I haven't eaten all day. I've been too nervous knowing I was going to see Derek again. But I'm not hungry at the thought of him doing whatever the hell it is that he does. My mind is going wild with speculations of what that "business" is.

"You know why I was drawn to you?" Derek breaks my thoughts as the waiter leaves us alone again.

"You had this sweetness about you. You didn't let others ruin it." His words take me back. My heart seemingly beating slower, and my body heating in the best of ways.

"I remember seeing that chick. She was a bitch." He makes a face like he's trying to remember her name, but it doesn't come to him. "Some preppy bitch at school made fun of you because you had a knockoff purse." I instantly know who he's talking about. Scarlett Dubet, and it was a fake Dooney and Bourke my aunt had given me. And yeah, she was a bitch with a capital "B".

"You just ignored her, but I knew it hurt you. Then a few weeks later, she dropped her purse in the parking lot as she was getting out of her car. All her shit went everywhere," Derek says and gestures with his hands. "You didn't even hesitate to go over and help her pick her things up. All I could think was I need to meet that girl, because who wouldn't want someone that sweet in their life?" he tells me as he grabs my hand softly, moving it to the bit of space between us on the bench and staring into my eyes.

The air between us is so intense, I have to look away.

I can't believe he remembers that. I haven't thought about her in years, but yeah, I remember helping that bitch pick her books up. I hated how mean she always was. I know her clique talked about me behind my back too. I didn't run in their circle, and I was okay with that, but all her stuff was getting soaked. There were still puddles all over from the morning rain. So yeah, I helped. I think anyone would have.

I swallow the lump growing in my throat. That was a few weeks before we first talked.

I also remember turning around to see him staring at my ass. Needing to lighten the mood, I call him on it.

"Oh really, is that what you were thinking? As I recall," I pause to pull my hand away from his and grab my glass of wine, playing with the stem a bit before picking it up. "You were staring at my ass as I was bent over helping her," I say confidently before taking a sip of the sweet wine.

Derek laughs. God, I love the sound of his laugh. It's rougher than it should be. Deeper and all man. I could listen to him laugh all day.

"Wow," he says, shaking his head and picking up his own glass. "Here I am, being all romantic and sweet for you, and you have to go and ruin it," he says, pretending to be offended. I love this playful side of him. This is the man I want. The side of him I looked forward to all those years ago.

"Yeah, yeah. You just want to get a piece, just like you did back then," I say with a flirtatious grin.

"I can't believe you said that. You need to be punished for that smart mouth of yours." His voice gets harder, carrying more than a hint of reprimand and my heart stammers. "Get underneath the table," he commands, his eyes piercing into me.

"What?" I ask, not believing what he just said. I can't even breathe as he holds my gaze without blinking. He's gotta be fucking kidding.

"Do it," he commands again.

"Are you out of your fucking mind?" I practically hiss. I am not getting under the table. But my thighs involuntarily clench at the thought of him punishing me. I hide my face behind my hand and try not to be turned on by the image of going down on him right now. What the fuck is wrong with me?

"Not now, the waiter's coming," he says in a more light-hearted tone, smirking at me.

I look up at him, face flushed with my heart racing, and my clit throbbing with need.

He smiles broadly. "You were really thinking of doing it?" he asks with disbelief.

Oh, you fucker. I bite down on my lip, feeling a bit of outrage stirring inside me, but mostly relief.

He starts laughing, and I can't help but swat him on his arm. It feels good to be this relaxed with him.

He shrugs and says, "I just wanted to see how you'd react." I smack him again playfully and settle into the leather-lined booth.

"You didn't seem to mind me going down on you the other night," he says after the waiter sets down our plates and refills our wine glasses, then leaves.

"I was high." I say the words a little louder than I should, and I instantly cover my mouth.

"And you liked it," he says with a wink.

I feel the blood rushing to my face, making my cheeks burn. *Who wouldn't?* He can't hold that against me.

"Come on sweetheart, you know I'll take care of you after," he goads.

"Shut up," I say playfully, sneaking a glance at him as I spear my fork into the risotto. I close my eyes, savoring the delicious flavor, but they pop open just as quickly as they closed at the sound of breaking glass.

"You stupid bitch!" echoes throughout the restaurant, and the place goes silent. The only sound is the scraping of wooden chair legs across the tiled floor as a man in a grey suit with a crisp white shirt pushes back from his seat and stands up. He's wiping furiously down his shirt with his white cloth napkin and cursing as he does.

Everyone turns to see what's happening. Across from him is another man who's not doing a damn thing to stop the shit-show this guy is putting on.

"I'm so-" a waitress is standing next to the man, mortified and clearly upset. She's bent over the table, picking up the wine bottle and a glass that's fallen onto the floor and shattered.

"Sorry! Do you know how much this suit cost?" the man screams at her.

That poor waitress! My heartbeat quickens watching him stare her down as she picks up the plates with the spilled wine.

"Sir, I do apologize," the maître d' begins as he walks up to the pissed off patron, but the customer takes a step forward and gets right in the guy's face.

Oh shit. My body heats as I watch this guy freak the fuck out.

"It's all on the house," the waitress says shakily.

What a fucking prick!

I glance at Derek, and the look on his face is murderous. His pale eyes are smoldering, and his strong jaw is tightly clenched.

"Derek," I say but I barely get his name out before he climbs out of the booth, my hand on his arm does nothing to stop him.

I scoot out of the booth after him, the sound of the man yelling dimming as the blood rushes in my ears.

Fuck. This isn't good.

CHAPTER 8

Derek

Adrenaline is coursing through my blood, and all I can see is my father. I'm breathing heavy, and my fist is screaming in pain. My knuckles split from the impact of landing the punch right to this fucker's jaw.

Don't fucking talk to her like that! I can hear myself scream as my father tries to hit her again. It's all I can see. How I was helpless back then. But now, watching the same scene play out, I'm not going to sit back and watch.

I can't allow it. I can't fucking stand a man yelling at a woman. A man putting his hands on her, talking down to her. Degrading her and making her scared.

I won't allow it.

The table rattles and the glass clinks as the other man at the table jolts back, his chair hitting the floor as he stands and backs away slowly.

My body's tense and ready for a fight.

The waitress steps back, and so does everyone else. I can feel their eyes on me as the fucker lands hard on the tiled floor. He throws one hand up in surrender while the other cups his jaw. His mouth fills with blood. All I can see is red.

"I-" The fucker on the ground cowers and starts to speak, but I yank him up by his collar. Every inch of my skin covered with a cold sweat as my heart pounds.

"Apologize," I scream in his face. I clench my jaw so tight, I think my teeth crack. I'm so on edge.

"Derek." I can faintly hear Emma's small voice, laced with fear. My grip loosens for a moment, my heart skipping a beat. Shame momentarily cripples me.

"I'm sorry," the man in my grasp says to the waitress on my left.

"I'm alright." I hear the waitress's voice. She's talking to the maître d', who's consoling her a bit to my left and behind me. Not this prick.

I know her. I forget her name, but I know her story. She's a friend of the Marianis. She lost her husband recently, and is just trying to get by. She's new, and she fucked up. But she didn't deserve that. And this asshole being so comfortable doing this in public means he's done it before.

I'm gonna make sure he never does it again.

"Derek," Emma calls out a little louder, desperation clearly there. I see her walk closer to us in my periphery. I hesitate. She shouldn't see this shit.

"Stay there, Emma," I tell her sharply. I swallow thickly, wishing I could just take this shit out on him. He deserves it.

"I'm sorry, just-" The guy says; he's shaking so hard I swear he's gonna piss himself. Just the sound of his voice pisses me off.

"Derek, stop!" Emma calls out again, taking a step forward and reaching out for my arm.

My anger wanes as my concern for her getting in the middle of us grows, but it's still there, raging inside of me.

"Get the fuck out," I say beneath my breath and start to shove him away, back against the wall. But it's not enough. I haul his ass out of the restaurant, not letting go of the grip I have on his shirt. I'm walking so fast he struggles to keep up.

As soon as we're outside, I shove him forward. The cold bitter air chilling my heated skin. He slips on the thin sheet of snow, landing hard onto his knees, the palms of his hands bracing his fall and a small splatter of blood hitting the pure white sidewalk.

I get a strong urge to kick the fucker right in his ribs. I want him to hurt. I want him to feel this for a long fucking time, but Emma runs out like a fucking madwoman, right in front of me. She's wearing her coat and has her wristlet in hand, with my coat draped over one arm.

I grit my teeth and grab hold of her waist to pull her behind me.

"Stop!" she screams at me.

What's she doing? *She should know better.*

The sounds of the people coming out of the restaurant and stirring around me barely grab my attention as the man hobbles forward and turns on his side to stand up. I give him a look that should fucking kill, and he freezes on the sidewalk.

"Please Derek, let's go. Just stop." Emma sounds so hurt as she pulls on my arm. "Please," she says and her soft voice grabs my full attention as she tugs at me again, pulling my shirt tighter across my chest. "Let's go."

Her beautiful doe eyes look up at me. My heart slows. It's only then I realize how heavy I'm breathing. How cold it is.

The man on the ground coughs and scoots farther away. I spare him a quick look, but nothing more.

"Let's go," Emma pleads as she tugs on my arm again, and

this time I go to her, shrugging on my coat easily. I wrap my arm around her waist and walk us toward my car. Emma looks over her shoulder a few times, but I don't. My pace is fast. I just want to get the fuck out of here.

Mariani's will be fine. The other owners have done worse. She doesn't need to know that though.

She tries to open the passenger door, but I push her against it instead. Her back hits the car door and she gasps as I press my body against hers.

I just wanna feel her. I need to.

"Derek," she whimpers, moving her neck to give me more access as I lean against her. Kissing her exposed skin, I push my knee between her legs. Fuck, I want her so bad. My dick starts hardening at the thought of taking her right here, right now. I'm so worked up. And I've wanted her for days. Fuck that. *Years.*

My heavy breath turns to fog as I leave open-mouth kisses along her neck.

"Derek," she says again in little more than a whisper, pushing me away slightly.

I don't expect her to push me away, since she was leaning into me at first. But she looks over her shoulder at the entrance to the Bistro and then back at me, that vulnerability in her eyes again.

I pull away and open the door for her without another word. Waiting for her to climb in, I can hardly look her in the eyes, before I shut it gently and readjust my cock in my jeans.

I look back at the restaurant one last time, the bright red blood still visible from this far away.

I shouldn't have done that.

I just can't allow a man to treat a woman like that. But the way Emma's pushing me away makes it more than obvious I shouldn't have done that.

It's quiet in the car. Too fucking quiet. The small cuts on my knuckles are irritating the shit out of me as I drive on the interstate, taking us closer to my house, and her sister's.

I don't want to end the night like this. I want her to come home with me. I wanna make it up to her. I twist my hand on the wheel and swallow down my pride.

"I'm sorry," I finally say, my voice rough and low. I'm staring straight ahead, but I can feel those beautiful hazel eyes on me. I chance a look at her and she doesn't seem angry, or disappointed. Instead there's a different look in her eyes, the same look she gave me that first day all those years ago. Like she's trying to figure me out. Trying to decide who I am.

"He was a dick," she finally says, ignoring my apology. My skin tingles with an uncomfortable heat as we get closer to the off ramp. My heart is clenching tight in my chest.

"Yeah. You okay?" I ask her.

"I'm fine," she answers quickly. She finally sits back in her seat a bit, but she still looks tense.

"I mean it," I say and look at her and wait for her eyes to meet mine. "I'm sorry."

Her expression softens and she puts her small hand on my lap, leaning toward me slightly.

"It's alright," she says softly. But that look is still in her eyes.

"I want you, Sweetheart." I look back toward the road, and realize I have to decide soon where I'm taking her. "Come home with me tonight."

"I'm not like that." She shakes her head a bit and pulls away from me. "I'm really sorry I gave you that impression."

"Like what?"

"Just an easy lay," she answers absently.

"Where the fuck did that come from?" I ask her with some of my anger coming through. Before she can answer, I continue. "I've wanted you since high school. I don't fuck around. I don't let people in. But you're there. Somehow I never had a choice on whether or not I could let you in."

"It's just that I'm going back-" Emma starts to say, but I'm shutting that shit down. She can tell me she hates what I do, over and over again. I can live with that. But I won't let her think that she's just an easy lay for me. Joking around? Sure. But actually believing it? No. She better fucking not.

"This isn't me thinking you're a one-night stand. *I want you.*" I emphasize the last part and feel a prickling sensation along my skin as she stares back at me. I can see she's deciding whether or not she believes me. I've never given her any reason not to, but it's been so long. I still feel everything from back then as if it was yesterday. I can only hope she does, too.

"Just give me the night to convince you," I plead with her. I know I fucked tonight up. I know she's worried about the shit I do, and the man I am. But I just need her touch. "Don't think about anything else. It's just you and me right now."

I turn the car onto the exit ramp, and now I have to go one of two ways. Left takes me home; right takes me to her sister's.

"Just tonight?" I ask her, keeping my car in the left lane, but looking behind me in the rearview, ready to steer the car to the right if she tells me to.

Finally, she nods and answers, "Just tonight." My body relaxes slightly, the adrenaline still coursing through me.

I have her for the night. If nothing else, I have her for tonight.

CHAPTER 9

Emma

My body feels so hot, and then so cold, alternating between the two and leaving me feeling helpless. I've never felt so anxious, so uncomfortable before. So worried. My fingers touch the dip in my throat as I glance at Derek and then back out of the window.

Derek's calmed down some, but I haven't. How can he be so at ease after what just happened?

The guy had it coming to him, but it was just so intense.

I look out of the window and watch all of the beautiful houses pass by as he drives us through his neighborhood. They put my sister's house to shame.

I'm barely taking them in though. I'm too worked up and on edge, preoccupied with visions of him gripping that asshole by the collar and lifting him nearly off the ground.

I've never seen him like that.

I've never seen *anyone* like that.

I don't like it. It was sexy as fuck in some ways. But it scares me. *He* scares me. I swallow thickly, closing my eyes at the realization.

I've always known he was a bad boy. I've only ever had glimpses though. I don't like seeing it up close and personal. I don't want it to be true.

We pull into Derek's driveway, my thoughts paused as I wait with bated breath to get out.

I couldn't tell him no. What's worse is that, even with a hint of fear, I still want him. Maybe even more now than I did before.

He gets out first and I move to open my door, but he motions for me to stop.

Sagging back in my seat, I watch as he walks around the front of the car. I take a deep breath and try to calm my nerves. I'm completely head over heels for him, even after what just happened. Ever since I walked away from him, I've never felt the way I had when we were together, and I'm terrified to lose it again. To never feel that way again for the rest of my life.

Fear of loss is making me cling to him.

I'm so fucked. This is all just fucked.

He opens my door and offers me his hand. I accept it with a soft smile although there's hesitation in my action. I find myself looking at his knuckles, wanting to see if it's the one he bruised and cut, but it's not.

He squeezes my hand, and it calms me down. The door clicks shut, and the cold makes me unconsciously step even closer to him. He makes me feel delicate and protected.

This is the side of him that I know. This gentle side that treats me as if I deserve the world. This is the man I know, but there's more to him.

I want to know all of him. Not just the small part he's willing to show me.

I don't know if he'll ever open up though. The thought makes my heart pang in my chest.

Is it so bad that I want to help him? I feel like I can. Like it's what I was meant to do.

But only if he'll let me. He needs to want to change.

Right now's not the time for that though.

I just want to hold him and for things to fall back into place.

Just for tonight.

I'm too conflicted to deal with all of this right now. I don't know what's right and what's wrong, or what the fuck I'm doing.

The sound of my heels clicking on the pavement is muted by the thin layer of fresh snow as we walk up the cement path to his front porch.

Once we get inside, Derek sets his keys down on the table to the left of the door. The white rectangular table almost blends in with the walls. He helps me out of my coat as I continue to look around. Slate floors lead into a hallway beyond the open staircase. The light from the glass and iron pendant chandelier glimmers on the walls and ceiling. His place is amazing.

But it's drug money. My eyes close tight and my heart thuds to a halt. I think. I don't know.

"Stop thinking about it, Emma," he says as he hangs our coats on cast iron hooks by the door, as if he could read my mind just now. I don't answer him, although for some reason I feel guilty.

He leads me up the open staircase. All the while I can't look at him, my heart beating so fast. I'm too nervous to even touch the railing, although without his hand on my back I'm not sure I'd be able to walk steadily.

I know I have a choice right now, to stay and be with him, or to leave. I need to decide right now. But I can't. I can hardly breathe. I hate that I'm just going with it, falling deeper into whatever it is we have. It's all I've ever done, but it's also all I want.

The black steel-frame lamp turns on automatically as we walk into the spacious bedroom. He lets go of my hand and walks into the en suite bathroom. I stare at the bed. It has to be a king with how large it is. The dark grey comforter has silver threading that gleams in the soft lighting. My heart thuds over and over again, the blood rushing in my ears.

I'm hot and ready for him. I want *this*. But it comes with so much. It means so much more to me.

And what does it mean to him?

"Make yourself at home," he calls out as he turns on the faucet.

I slowly walk over and sit down in the navy armchair in the corner of the room, the bathroom and therefore Derek, visible from my seat.

His room is so masculine, so *him*. But it's devoid of warmth. It's missing a crucial piece of him. The piece he gives to me.

The smoky grey walls are bare, the only picture sitting on the nightstand. A little boy and a young mother smile together as they pose on top of the mountain they just climbed. *It must be Derek and his mom*, I think as I squint slightly to make out the picture across the room better.

I can't just sit here. I get up quickly, my blood feeling as though it's on fire, and cross the room to his bathroom. Derek's opening a bottle of peroxide to pour on the cuts on his knuckles.

"Let me help you," I say as I walk across the white marble floor. I take the bottle from him without waiting for a response and slowly pour the solution over his hand. His hand is so large and rough to the touch. I like holding it though. I like the abrasive feel. I concentrate on tending his knuckles. The cuts aren't as bad as I would have guessed from the way he was hitting that guy, and the blood that was there.

But that may not have been his blood.

"You really beat the piss out of him," I say as I twist the cap back onto the bottle. My heart feels like it's in my throat.

His eyes are on the floor as he says, "Yeah." He leans against the sink, his gaze occasionally flicking to mine, but I don't look back.

"You didn't have to, you know," I tell him, trying not to sound like I'm scolding him. I squeeze some Neosporin onto his knuckles as he sighs and then grunts a response.

I wait, staring up at him and willing him to look at me, but he doesn't.

"I know," he says quietly as he shakes his head.

"So why'd you do it?" I can't help but to ask him. Asking is the way to get answers. I know that from my classes and from working with the kids at school. I hate comparing Derek to them, but he's like them in so many ways. Right now, all I want to do is help him.

I lay the gauze over his bloodied knuckles and wrap the medical tape around his hand while I wait for him to answer me, but nothing comes.

Derek looks like he's not going to tell me anything, and I shake my head feeling my throat go dry. I can't do this. I can't be with someone who won't talk to me. I clean up the first aid kit and put it back in the cabinet under the double sinks, not speaking as he moves out of the way.

"He reminded me of my father," he says before I can walk out of the bathroom. I stop in the doorway, waiting for more.

"Your father?" I ask him. He only ever told me about his father once. That he'd left them, but that's all I know. He never wanted to talk about his family.

I look over my shoulder, gripping the door in my hand

and I can see the hatred and pain in his eyes. Seeing him like this feels like I'm being stabbed in the chest. I just want to hold him and take his pain away, but I need to understand.

I walk back in and lean against the granite countertop. It's cold under my hand, but I'd rather touch it than him. If he holds me, I'll lose focus. I'll lose him opening up to me, and I can't do that. "I don't know anything about him," I tell him with a seemingly casual shrug.

"It's best that you don't."

"I wanna know." I *need* to know.

"He wasn't a good man. Like that fucker at the restaurant…" He trails off and shakes his head. "The things he was saying," Derek shakes his head again, closing his eyes. "No woman should be talked to that way."

"Your dad talked to your mom like that?" I ask.

"Yeah, right before he'd beat her," he says, and I can hear the raw hurt in his voice. My heart breaks for him and I could just cry. I move closer to him and grab his unbandaged hand. I can't resist touching him.

"I'm sorry," I say quietly. I reach my hand to his chest, waiting for him to look me in the eyes. "Is she alright?" I ask him.

His eyes flash with something I can't place.

"He's gone now," he answers, but it feels like something else. Like he's hiding more from me.

"I want to know you, Derek," I plead with him.

He huffs a humorless laugh and swallows thickly, looking behind me and into the mirror before returning my gaze. "I think you're the *only* one who knows me."

I don't know what to say to that. It can't be true. "That'd be a shame if that's true." I speak without thinking. I know who he is--I know his character, his soul, but I don't know his story.

"Shame? Yeah." He nods, looking behind me again. "Yeah, maybe it is."

He grips my waist, setting me on the edge of the counter and leans in closer to me so we're the same height. His eyes are filled with such sadness. I wish I could take it away. I want the playfulness back. I want him to be happy.

He rests his forehead against mine and barely kisses me, his lips just brushing mine, leaving me wanting more.

My thumb rubs circles on the back of his hand as we stand in silence.

Finally, he breaks the moment with another deep sigh. It's been a stressful night.

"I've got problems, Emma. You know that. But I still want you. Just stay with me?" he pleads.

I close my eyes, hating the way he talks about himself. It makes me think about all the lessons I took, learning how to react to low self-esteem in my classes. Preparing me to work with schools and be a guidance counselor. The psychology of it is why I got into it.

But right now those are just words on a page.

I cup his jaw in my hand and bring my lips up to his.

"Everyone has problems. You just need someone to lean on," I whisper.

I desperately want to be that person, but I'm scared. I'm more than that, I'm terrified. I'm so close to the edge of a deep abyss. I feel like I barely made it out unscathed last time. And we were just kids. Now I know what it feels like to not have him.

I want him just as much as he wants me, but for me, there's no turning back. It's all or nothing.

His hands slip up my dress, his bare skin touching mine in a soft caress that leaves goosebumps in his path.

My nipples pebble, and my breath hitches.

"Derek," I say but I barely get his name out, lost in the soft feel of his touch. He's always so gentle with me. Forceful in some ways, but I feel like I can tame the beast inside of him. It's a heady feeling. It's intoxicating.

"Just feel me, Emma," he whispers back, pushing his lips against mine. I'm hesitant at first, not sure if I should take this leap. I'm already weak for him; this will only put me over the edge. "Let me feel you."

He nips my bottom lip gently then brushes the tip of his nose against mine.

"I want you," he says just above a murmur. I can't resist him. I've never been able to tell him no.

"I bet you're already wet for me," he whispers against the shell of my ear as he reaches below, his hand cupping my pussy. I am. I know I am. I'm hot and wet and desperate for him.

He groans, the sexiest fucking sound I've ever heard, deep and rough and primal. "Such a good girl, Sweetheart."

His dirty words make me blush, my skin heating and every nerve ending on edge. He pulls my dress over my head and tosses it carelessly to the floor before slipping off my high heels. They land on the floor, clacking against the tile, one and then the other.

"I want you to watch," he says as he turns me around to face the mirror, my bare feet against the cold tile, and the granite counter against my hips.

My body tingles and heats with an intensity I can barely stand. I close my eyes…I can't watch.

"Keep them open," he says. My eyes pop open and find his in the mirror.

The sound of his jeans unzipping and then falling to the floor makes my breathing come in frantic pants. He holds my gaze as his thumbs rip through the thin lace of my panties and he lets them drop to the floor.

"I want to hear you scream my name, Sweetheart," he

whispers, his head leaning against mine and his breath tickling my neck.

I can hardly feel the sensation though. My pussy is hot and pulsing with need as I feel him pressing into my pussy. The head of his cock pushes gently through my folds, back and forth.

"You're so wet for me, sweetheart," he breathes, making me hotter and wetter, frenzied for his touch.

I close my eyes as he brushes against my clit. My hard nipples peak, and my head falls back against his hard chest.

"Open, Emma," he commands me and the second I obey, he slams into me. All the way to the hilt. Filling me, and stretching my walls. I instantly bend over, my body tense with a heated sensation so sudden my breath is caught in my throat. There's a hint of pain, mixed with intense pleasure as my hands grip the counter. His eyes pierce into mine in the reflection. Forcing me to stare back as he pounds into me again and again, jolting my body. Holy fuck.

My voice is gone; I desperately want to scream out my pleasure, but my body is in shock, paralyzed from his demanding touch. He doesn't hold back. Savagely fucking me, without any mercy. His hot body's pressed against mine and it's the only thing keeping me up right.

His hand grips my right hip, holding me in place as he fucks me harder with a steady pace. He finally closes his eyes, reaching his other hand up to grip my throat. The bandaged hand. He kisses me gently on the crook of my neck. It's so at odds with the way he fucks me.

"Derek," I finally get out his name as he pounds into me. He does it again. And again. Each time pushing my pleasure higher, making my body sing with a tingling heat that makes it hard to stand. My fingers slip against the counter and then grip onto his hand at my throat.

My eyes want to close, but I can't.

He groans with pleasure into my ear as his pace picks up.

"I knew you'd feel like this," he says as he pushes his thick cock even deeper and harder, my left hip slamming against the counter with a bruising force. The pleasure stirs in my belly, rising higher and higher, consuming me more and more.

The pain doesn't even register, it only pushes me closer to that forbidden edge. I'm so high up, I feel as though I'll shatter when he sends me crashing over.

"Derek!" I scream his name as he holds himself deep inside of me, pushing against my walls and stealing the breath from my lungs.

So close, I'm so fucking close. I claw at his wrist, desperate for more, but afraid at the same time.

He kisses my cheek so gently, his eyes on mine, and then the small moment breaks and he fucks me like he owns me.

He's slamming himself into me over and over. Taking his pleasure from me with a ruthless need. His hand reaches in front of me, and his fingers strum my clit.

His merciless touch sends me flying even higher. It's my undoing, and pushes me over the edge in a rush, every nerve ending in my body firing at once. My body goes limp, but he holds me in place, rutting between my legs and racing for his own release as my orgasm rips through my body.

My vision goes black as I fall against him, my head resting on his shoulder and my body jolting with each hard thrust of his hips until he cums deep inside of me. I feel his cock pulsing, and his hot cum filling me.

It's everything I've ever wanted.

Everything I've ever feared.

And now it's done.

CHAPTER 10

Derek

I WAKE up with a yawn and the early morning light in my face. I crack my neck and stretch one arm over my head, feeling the pull of the muscle down my shoulders and back.

Only one arm though, since my sweetheart is sleeping on the other. Her head rests on my bicep. My arm's sore and stuck under her weight, but I don't want to move.

She looks so innocent in her sleep. She's too beautiful to disturb, too peaceful.

I lay my head back and stare at the ceiling. I'm such a selfish fuck.

But she feels so good. So right.

I know I'm not any good for her, but I'm not willing to just let her go. I know what it feels like to lose her. I don't want to feel that ever again. I'll lie, cheat, steal, whatever the fuck I have to do to keep her.

I'll make it up to her. I'll keep all the bad shit at arm's length and as far away from her as I can.

I can do that for her.

I turn my head back to her and gently kiss her hair. She sighs softly, nestling into me.

A small smile hits my lips. I can't help what she does to me. Just being with her makes me feel like a better person, like I can be a better man. She's always made me feel that way though, even now when I know I can't.

I gently pry her off of me, scooting away as quietly as I can. She responds with a soft moan of protest in her sleep before rolling over.

I wait with bated breath as she turns her back to me, restlessly settling into the comforter trying to get comfortable until she's still and her breathing steadies.

I'd love to watch her all day, but I need to feed my sweetheart. I want to keep her happy and make sure she doesn't regret this.

I'm quiet as I sneak out of the room, careful not to disturb her more than I have to. I take one last look as I carefully open the door, the soft creak making her stir in her sleep.

The only other person in the house is Ma. I'm used to making the two of us breakfast, although lately she hasn't had much of an appetite. The thought makes me feel uneasy as I make my way down the stairs.

Ma's room is much closer to the kitchen than the upstairs bedrooms; I'm sure she'll hear me as soon as I start cooking. I get the pans out, making as little noise as possible. Heating up the first skillet, I grab butter and eggs and get to work. It's not long until I hear a noise behind me, before I can even get the first plate ready.

I turn to look over my shoulder as I crack another egg on the side of the pan.

I thought Emma was beautiful in her sleep, but the way

her hair is gently mussed, making her look well-fucked, combined with the sleepy look still in her eyes... she's more radiant now than I've ever seen her.

I could wake up to her every morning. "Do you eat?" I ask her.

She huffs a small laugh, tucking her hair behind her ears as she leans against the wall to the doorway and finally looks up at me. "Yeah, I eat." There's a small smile to her lips that makes my chest swell with pride.

I give her a cocky smirk as I say, "I thought you might."

I turn my back to her, getting back to the eggs and flipping them. "You want to grab the bacon out of the fridge, Sweetheart?"

I hear the soft pad of her feet as she walks behind me on the tiled kitchen floor. I can't get over this feeling that she's going to leave me. That I'm not good enough, and I need to work harder to keep her. I don't know how to make it go away.

"Are you going to cook for me?" Emma asks with a hint of humor. I turn to see Emma close the fridge door by pushing it with her hip.

"I like to cook." I shrug as I answer her. It's true. It's always been a hobby of mine. Ma says she used to watch the cooking channel when she was pregnant with me. She couldn't get enough of those shows. She thought I was meant to be a chef. I don't know about all that, but I fucking love food. Who doesn't?

"Well, I could definitely get used to that," Emma says as she puts the package of bacon on the counter. She stands there next to me for a moment without saying or doing anything, just looking at me. I can tell she's a little uncomfortable, wondering where all this is going.

"Could you now?" I ask her playfully, trying to put her at

ease. She looks up at me with those beautiful eyes of hers, a soft smile on her lips.

"It depends on what you want in return." Her voice is breathy and flirtatious, making my dick stir in my pants. I have to readjust myself and ignore the pan to turn and face her. Damn, the things she does to me. There's just something about a good girl being bad for me that makes me want to move the world for her. But I don't have time to respond. Instead a noise behind us distracts both of us. It's Ma.

She stands in the doorway for a moment, still in her pajamas. They're made of a thin fabric, just pants and a long-sleeve grey shirt. They make her look more frail, hanging so loosely from her body. I look between the two women, feeling nervous all of a sudden. I don't know how they're going to react to each other. Ma moved in a few months ago, and she's never seen me with a woman. Not that I haven't been with them, I've just never brought them home before. Emma's different though. It's best to just get this shit out of the way.

"Ma, this is Emma." I turn back to the pan and talk with my back to both of them. "We didn't mean to wake you." I'm sure she was already up anyway. But I'm trying to keep the conversation light.

"Emma?" Ma says her name as if she knows who she is already. As if she's trying to place her in her memory. But they never met before back when we were a secret. I never introduced Emma to anyone.

"Hi." Emma's sweet voice comes out soft. She shifts a little before walking to the island and nervously taking a seat. She seems so shy as I glance over my shoulder to take her in. It reminds me of the first day I met her. Always quiet, that pureness about her shining through.

"Oh yes, I remember you." Ma looks at Emma with a small smile on her face. The look in her eyes is one I haven't seen in a very long time. Like she's up to something. "Derek used to give you a ride to school."

My brow furrows. I didn't think Ma had ever seen us together back then. "Nah, I used to give her a ride home sometimes though," I say, scratching the back of my head and wondering what all Ma saw.

"That could be. All I know is that I could've sworn you two were going to get into trouble in the back of your car."

I look over at Emma, the sizzling of the pan filling out the awkward silence in the room.

Emma clears her throat, a violent blush on her cheeks. "It's nice to meet you, Mrs. Wade."

"It's nice to *finally* meet you, too." Ma takes a few steps forward and I leave the stove to try to help her walk into the kitchen and toward the island, but she shoos me away. "It took him long enough."

"The first time I saw you I thought you were bad news." Emma's eyes go wide as she listens to Ma. I grunt a laugh.

"I think you got a few things mixed up," I mutter, plating the eggs and putting the bacon in the pan on the back of the stove. I add more butter to the first pan and wait for it to melt.

"I saw you sneak around the back of the house." I tilt my head, looking at Ma as I set the knife down on the counter. There's no way she saw us back then. She used to yell at me all the time about the shit I was into. I'll never forget how guilty she made me feel when I first started selling. I had to lie to her. I kept everything from her. I was careful about it so I wouldn't break her heart.

It would kill her if she knew. Even today she'll swear up and down it's my father who gave me a bad reputation. She'd go to her grave thinking I'm taking the fall for him. She has no idea.

I ignore the guilt growing in my chest and turn back to

the stove, my heart clenching just knowing the pain it would cause her if she found out. I did what I had to do. She thinks I made extra money working at the factory. She didn't know I was selling dope out of the back. I'll never tell her, and I'll kill any prick who even thinks about spreading the fucked up truth to her.

"You always thought you were getting away with everything, Derek." Ma points her finger at me, shaking it slightly, but there's a smile on her face. "Back then I knew a little. Maybe I'm losing it now, but back then I was onto you."

Emma's face is bright red, but a smile is plastered on her lips. "I promise you, I had the best intentions," Emma says just as comically as Ma, with her hand on her heart. I shake my head, looking between the two of them. Emma raises her voice as she says, "I swear we never did anything."

"And now?" Ma asks.

"And now what?" Emma asks.

"What are you two doing now?"

"Ma!" Jesus. No wonder I never brought a girl home.

Ma shrugs, a smug look on her face. Emma's hiding behind a hand in front of her face, her shoulders shaking with silent laughter, and she can't look either of us in the eyes.

My mother takes a few steps to the stool. She's nearly out of breath by the time she gets there and Emma's quick to help get her steady on the stool. There's a back to it, but even with that, it's bar height and I'm not sure she should be sitting on it.

"You sure you want to be up there? I can bring breakfast to your room." I stand behind my mother, my hand on the back of her chair as I set a plate in front of her. It's just eggs, but usually she's able to eat eggs without any nausea.

"I like it out here just fine," Ma says, a little out of breath although she's trying to hide it.

Emma looks between the two of us, and I can tell she's not sure what to think. She has no idea Ma has cancer, that she's not doing well; but it's more than obvious she's not healthy. She looks so much older than she is. I wish I'd introduced them back when we were in high school. Looking at the worry in Emma's eyes, I know I should've told her about Ma. I'm gonna have to explain it later.

"You could've told me you had a girl, Derek," Ma says as she spears a fork into her eggs.

I that she looks fragile and weak compared to the strong woman I remember her as.

It's been a long time since I've actually looked at her. Like really looked at her.

Ma puts her fork down next to her plate, and the silver clinks against the ceramic as her hand shakes. "Could you grab me a cup of milk, dear?" Ma sets her elbow on the table, resting her head in her hand.

This happened the other day, too. Eating's been taking a lot out of her. I don't know if the chemo is making her nauseated, if she's just not sleeping enough, or if something else is going on.

Before I can move to the fridge, Emma's already there. She grabs the milk quickly with a serious look on her face.

Setting the jug on the counter, she opens up one cabinet door and then the next and the next.

"Right here, Sweetheart." I open up the cabinet door closest to my right and grab a large plastic cup, handing it over to Emma.

"Thank you," she says softly.

She pours a cup of milk without looking at me.

"Ma, you sure you don't want to go to your room?" I ask, my hand on her shoulder. "You could lie down. Or maybe the booth in the dining room nook?" I added a bench in there up against the wall, and near the window. She likes sitting in there to read and get some sun. She shouldn't be sitting up here on the stool with how unsteady she is. I can just picture her falling off.

She puts her small hand on mine, and it's cold. She pats my hand a few times and nods her head. "I think I should go back to bed. "She swallows thickly, and the happiness that was in her eyes vanishes. "I just thought I heard a new voice in this empty house."

"I can take you there if you want," Emma says softly. "You have to show me where though." Ma returns Emma's hesitant smile. "I can get there myself. I'll be alright. You just stay here and keep an eye on my boy." Ma turns to me and gives me a wink. "He needs someone out here keeping him in line."

CHAPTER 11

Emma

It's crazy how fast things change.

Two weeks ago, I was caught up in studying for school and thinking about my internship, planning for my future. I had checklists and everything mapped out. All I had to do was stay on the straight and narrow.

Now all I can think about is Derek. I'm second-guessing everything. I want to somehow fit him into all my plans, but he doesn't belong there.

It's just like it was back in high school. I'm willing to move everything around for him. The two of us fit together so well. We're meant to be; I can feel it. But the lives we lead don't blend.

As the days count down until I go back to school, it's getting harder and harder to ignore. It's nearly impossible to pretend everything is just fine and fall into his bed without any worries. The tick-tock, tick-tock of the proverbial clock never shuts the fuck up anymore. I shake my head as I grab my textbooks and head downstairs to the kitchen, pushing the awful truth away. Why can't life just be easy? Why are there these choices that make it so you can't have everything? Even as I question it, I know I'm being ridiculous.

After the other night, there's no way I can walk away from Derek again. But I don't see how we're going to make this work. Especially when we aren't even talking about it. He's not going to change, and I can't be with him and turn a blind eye forever.

I set my books on the kitchen table, grab myself a glass of orange juice, and sit down, ready to study. I just need to focus. A sigh leaves me in a long exhale as I push the hair out of my face.

As I open my book and start reading, my thoughts drift back to Derek. I can't stop thinking about all of the things he's going through, and how hard his life is compared to mine. He's only told me little bits and pieces. He never wants to talk about it. I get it. I do. But he needs someone. He has no one, and that's by choice. I don't understand how he doesn't see that. He has me, at least. I can see through his bullshit. But he's never going to be okay if he keeps it all bottled up.

My chest feels so tight and painful as I think about everything he's dealing with on his own. Watching his mom slowly being taken away by cancer. Tears prick my eyes, and I take in a heavy breath. I check my phone, merely looking for a distraction, even though I know I don't have any new messages.

It's been two days since I've seen him, but we've been texting back and forth. I miss him, which is a dangerous thing.

I stretch my arms and shake out all this tension before I get back to the task at hand and start reading. *Focus, Emma.*

I have to blink my eyes several times as the black words fade into the white pages. I read the words, but I can't remember a single fucking sentence. As I read the same paragraph over for the third time, I hear a knock on the door.

I instantly push the chair back, thankful for something to do other than this mindless shit, but Sandra calls down, "I'll get it!" as she's running down the steps. I grit my teeth and push my chair back in, putting my elbow on the table and resting my chin in my hand. I know I shouldn't. I break out on my chin sometimes from stress, and the oils from my hand doesn't help, but fuck it. I don't care.

As Sandra opens the door, I listen carefully, part of me hoping it's Derek.

"Hey baby," Tony says softly. Every time he greets her there's this softness in his voice that he only has for her. I must be emotional today, because just thinking about that makes those damn tears threaten to fall again.

"Hey!" Sandra says back happily. She doesn't understand how good she has it.

My hopes fall, and I try to concentrate on studying again. I'll see Derek and we'll talk about things soon. We need to, and both of us know that.

"Hi, Sandra." I instantly perk up at the sound of Derek's voice. It's him! My first instinct is to run to him like a freaking child. *Calm down, Emma. You don't want to scare him off. You're an adult.*

"Hey, Derek. Em's in the kitchen studying," Sandra answers.

"Ready to go?" Tony asks Sandra. Go? My heart speeds up, knowing we're going to have the house to ourselves. I'm not sure if these nerves are from knowing I'm falling for him all over again, or if it's because I'm already turned on just thinking about what we could do when we're all alone. It's weird having sex at his place with his mom there. It's only happened twice, but each time when it's over and I remember she's in the house I get this weird feeling like we just did something wrong. I wish I could drop it and just go with the flow, but I absolutely can't. It feels disrespectful in some sense. So instead we've been naughty in the car on the way back to his place or here. *Just like old times.*

"Em, I'll be home later! Love you!" Sandra yells down the hall on her way out of the house. "Bye, Derek. See you later," she says a little quieter.

"Love you!" I yell back. My response is followed by the sound of the door closing, and Derek's heavy footsteps in the hallway.

I get up to meet him and quickly smooth my hair before he enters the kitchen, butterflies in my stomach and my heart racing.

"Hi," Derek says with a smile as he enters the room. That smile. It brightens my world. I can't get enough of it. It's a crime that he doesn't smile all the time.

"Hi," I greet as I stand on my tiptoes, planting a kiss on his lips as he wraps his arms around my waist. "What are you doing here?" I ask, rocking on my feet.

He shrugs, looking past me for a moment and then back at me. "I have some time off, and I just wanted to hang out. Like we used to," he says as I wrap my arms around his neck. He leans in and kisses my neck. It's that sensitive place that somehow seems connected to both my nipples and clit. I'm already primed for him.

He walks us over to the chair I was sitting in before he got here, sits easily and pulls me onto his lap.

"You're on break, so take a break with me," he says as he closes my book.

I look into his eyes. We need to talk about what's happening here. I lick my lips as my blood pressure climbs, and suck it up. I'm a grown ass woman. We aren't two teens in puppy love. We're adults, and we need to talk.

"I'm scared, Derek," I say honestly. I think back to my lectures. State what you're feeling. Then explain why you're feeling it, and how you wish for it to be resolved. It's as simple as that.

"Of what, Sweetheart?" he says as he strokes my cheek. His eyes shine with sincerity, and a wrinkle forms right down the center of his forehead. It's always there when he's concerned. I trace it with my fingertip, wishing we didn't have to have this conversation. I shift in his lap, knowing it's for the best. Even if this isn't going to work, it's better that we get it out of the way now.

I close my eyes and clear my throat. "Of this, of us," I answer him.

He tucks a strand of hair behind my ear. "Don't think about it. Just go with it, Sweetheart." He kisses my neck again before I can respond, and I want to just go along with it. But I need to know what he's thinking, what we're doing here. I can't just keep brushing this under the rug.

"You know I'm going back soon. In three weeks," I say, pulling away to look him in the eye. A part of me thinks this is all just temporary for him anyway. As soon as I leave, he'll have someone else. It's a small part though. If I really believed it, it would make ending this so much easier. If I thought I could just be replaced so easily by him. But I don't think that. Maybe I'm naive, but I don't want to believe it.

His hands pause on my waist, his fingers gripping me a little tighter. "Yeah," he says suspiciously, that wrinkle returning.

"And then what?" I ask. That's really where my problem lies. I need to know.

"Well, it's only one semester, right?" he responds.

"Yeah." What is he thinking? I can feel that damn wrinkle

on his forehead form on mine. My heart seems to beat so loud that I can't hear anything else. I wish it would shut up. I need to hear what he's saying.

"That won't be long. Just a few months, and we can handle that," he says hopefully.

"I just don't want to start something, and then you go and fuck around-" the words come out so fast. I can't help it. It's what's in my head, and I need him to tell me it's going to be alright.

He grabs my face with both hands, forcing me to look at him. "I have never fucked around on you. I never will. I'm not interested in anyone else," he says, cutting me off. My breathing comes in faster.

"What is this between us?" I ask him. I stand up, pushing off his lap and getting out of his hold to put some space between us.

"I told you I want you." His voice is sincere as he grabs my hand, as if he needs to touch me to get through this.

"For now?"

He stands up and wraps his arms around my waist; I don't deny him. "For however long we have." I hate that answer. I need something more than that, something concrete. But the way he says it reminds me of what he's going through. I have to close my eyes and try to focus on our conversation, but I can't.

"Don't think about it, sweetheart. Just kiss me." His voice lowers as he pulls me closer to him.

I wish he would just say the words I'm thinking. *I love you.* It would make this so much easier. But that would be too good to be true. And I'm stupid for thinking it. *For however long we have.*

It's so easy to do as he says. To just stop thinking. The way he presses his lips to mine makes me want to forget about everything and just be his for the moment and I take them greedily, needing to just get lost in his touch.

Just this moment.

His hot tongue slips against the seams of my lips and part for him, opening and letting him inside my mouth. His tongue strokes strong and heavily against mine possessively. His kiss is taking from me with everything he has. It's a hot dark dance of our mingled breath.

As his hands roam my body, I realize that I'm enabling him. I'm allowing him to have me without any type of resolution. I'm weak because of him. I'm weak *for* him.

His fingers trail along my waist, tickling my skin and making me writhe under his touch. Such a soft touch. He's always gentle at first; that's how he gets me. He shows me the side of him that no one else can see.

It's a side I'm addicted to.

"Lie to me, sweetheart," Derek says as he pulls back, his eyes closed and his hot breath coming in quicker.

He lifts me up by the waist, walking the length of the small kitchen and setting me down on the counter. He kisses my neck gently as I register his words.

His lips barely press against the sensitive area just under my ear. *That spot.* He must know exactly what it does to me.

"Lie to you?" I ask. I'm surprised I can even talk, my heart's beating so fast and I feel like I can hardly even think.

His deft fingers unbutton my jeans, and I let him. I don't tell him no.

I can't. I want this just as much as he does, even if we haven't resolved a damn thing. He did say he'd never cheat on me. But how long is he mine to claim? And more importantly, when is he going to stop dealing? When is he going to straighten up his life?

I shake my head at the thought as he slips my jeans off my hips. He lifts my ass up off the counter and I have to lean against him, my arms wrapped around his shoulders. The denim slides down my thighs and he lowers himself while he pulls them off, kissing my collarbone, down between my breasts, down to my hips. He stops at my thighs, tugging the jeans down my legs.

They fall to the floor, making the only sound that fills the silence in the room besides our heavy breathing. "Lie to me and tell me I was your first," he says softly with his eyes on my pussy as he pushes my legs further apart.

He gently nips my thigh, his hands at the back of my knees as he gently kisses my leg, up to my hot pussy. He brushes his nose against my panties, and my cheeks flame with embarrassment. His hands move to my hips, holding me in place as he bites through the lace and gently nips my clit. *Fuck!* The heated sensation vibrates through my body.

My hands slide into his hair as I cry out, "Derek!" It's a sensation I've never felt before, a sharp pain followed by the sweet bliss of pleasure. I want it again. I want more; my clit throbs for more.

"Do it, Sweetheart," he says as he looks up at me with a hunger in his eyes I've never seen. He stares deep into my eyes as his thumbs tear through the lace of my panties, shredding them, making me bare to him. Holy fuck. "Tell me I was your first, I need to hear it."

He pulls my ass to the edge of the counter and lines his dick up; my legs wrap around his waist, my arms wrap around his shoulders. He kisses my throat and my head falls back as he gently pushes into me. I'm still sore. He's had me every day since he took me at his house.

"I can't," I say, shaking my head. We're already denying so much of the truth, but I won't lie to him. "I'll never lie to you, Derek."

He fills me so slowly, so sweetly, but with an aching stretch that burns slightly from his thick girth.

Derek's arms wrap around my back and one hand grips the nape of my neck as he thrusts harder into me. It's a punishing fuck, like he's angry I won't lie to him. I scream out loudly, not caring about anything. Just needing him to hear what he does to me.

"Lie to me, sweetheart," he groans through his clenched teeth as he continues to thrust harder and harder, pushing me higher and higher toward the peak I'm desperately seeking.

He forcefully pumps his hips over and over as his jeans fall to the floor around his ankles. He fucks me with primal need; my body heats, and my skin tingles with the sensation of desire. I need more. I whimper an incoherent response as I cling to him.

His rough pubic hair brushes against my clit with each stroke, making the intense feeling that much stronger. I feel so unsteady. Extreme pleasure stirs in the pit of my stomach and radiates outward. My toes seem to go numb as my fingers grip onto him, my nails digging through his thin t-shirt and into his shoulders. I bury my head in the crook of his neck as he continues the punishing fuck.

"Did he fuck you like this?" Derek asks, moving away from me slightly, but still buried deep in my heat, gripping my throat with his hand, forcing me to stare back at him. His blue eyes pierce into me.

"No," I say and shake my head, or at least I try to. I can barely function, paralyzed by the pleasure he's giving me.

"No one will ever fuck you like I can," he says in a low voice, and the intensity in his gaze is nearly too much. He reaches down with his other hand still squeezing my throat and pinches my clit again. My ass slams against the granite countertop, and the force of his thrusts are so strong that the dishes in the sink rattle. His fingers tighten around my throat although they don't constrict my breathing.

"Remember that, Emma," he says breathily. "I can give you this. I can give you what no one else can."

I grip onto him harder, the wetness between my thighs growing hotter. The sound of him pounding into me only makes him fuck me faster and harder as my arousal makes it easier for him. My heels dig into his ass as I hold onto him for dear life. The sensation numbs my body, heating it with a pleasure that threatens to consume me.

"I wish it had been you," I moan into the hot air between us tears pricking my eyes.

With the feeling of him taking from me so ruthlessly, savagely, devouring me with his hard merciless thrusts, I'm already so vulnerable. I'm already so weak and at his mercy. But I do wish it'd been him.

He's so rough with me I can hardly stand upright at the mixed sensations of pain and pleasure. He leans down, pushing my tank top and bra out of the way and sucks my nipple into his mouth, his teeth bite down and he pulls back. It hurts, but it's what sends me over. I spiral into a black abyss of paralyzing pleasure.

"It's my fault for letting you go." I barely hear Derek's whisper as he pushes himself inside me all the way to the hilt. I can barely stand the sensation as my head is thrown back, and a scream is ripped from my throat. He rubs my clit ruthlessly as my orgasm slowly radiates through my body, as if deliberately torturing me slowly with a pleasure so intense I can't fight it.

He cums with me, his thick cock pulsing and filling me. His cum spills from my pussy and down my thighs, mixing with the arousal that made it so easy for him to fuck me like that.

It's because I want him.

That's why he could take so much from me.

Because I'm so willing to give it to him.

CHAPTER 12

Derek

I RUN my fingers along the small silver pebbled frame sitting on the edge of my desk. It's a picture of me and Emma. It's been a couple of weeks, and Ma ordered me a picture frame. She said jokingly that I should have some evidence I could hold down a girl. I huff a laugh, remembering her jab. She thinks she's funny.

It's a good picture of the two of us, too. Emma had it; she kept it from all those years ago.

She took it in my car, lying next to me, holding her hand up as we lay across the back seats. The two of us are smiling. I can't think of another picture I have where I'm smiling unless it's forced. Ma used to make us get pictures together. She said it was important. I know she wanted me to get them because she thought she was dying. She wanted me to have a picture of the two of us, so I could remember her when she was gone.

In those pictures with her, I'm not really smiling. I hated getting them done. I only agreed to take them because I knew my ma needed them. I forced each smile for her. But they're not real.

I tap my finger against the edge of the silver picture frame.

Emma never showed me the pictures she took of us. I knew she wasn't gonna show anyone anyway, so it didn't matter to me. I didn't even know why she wanted them herself.

I'm glad she did though. Looking at the happiness in her eyes and the way I'm glancing at her rather than looking at the camera, I remember the way she made me feel back then. It's stronger now, which surprises me. It's hard to believe that I can feel more for her today than I did in high school. I guess things haven't changed much at all. We just picked up right from where we left off.

I think I remember that day, but there were so many of them where we did just that. Lay together in the back of my car, just holding each other and kissing. Some days I let my hands roam along her body.

A few times, she climbed on top of me. That's the most we ever did, when she'd grind against my hard cock. The first time she did it, I didn't even realize she was doing it on purpose. It drove me crazy, the slow grinding of her pussy against my dick.

The corners of my lips kick up into a small smile. I'll never forget that. I'll never let her forget that either. I made my good girl do bad things. I made her *want* bad things. I still do.

The days are flying by, but each day she seems to get more and more comfortable in my arms again. It helps that she isn't around any of the shit I'm doing. I sigh heavily, running my hands through my hair. I don't know how long I can keep this up. I'm putting off meets to go see her. I'm letting assholes get away with stupid shit, too. Which isn't a good look. Tony never fails to remind me of that.

Although if Emma saw the shit I'm doing today, she wouldn't have any concerns. I click on the mouse to get over to my emails again. It's just paperwork. All day I go through contracts for the businesses in my name. The legit ones. It's boring shit, but it needs to be done.

Everything is streamlined, but I still have my hand in every piece of the operation.

I didn't get far by handing off work to other people. The details are what matter. Being present matters. Every day I come to this office. Every problem goes through me. That's how it should be. I'm the boss, so I have to act the part. Everyone needs to know I'm here.

It's an important part of being respected. If I'm not doing the work, why would they even give a fuck about me? I could easily be replaced. I can handle the business end of the companies and restaurants I own all day long. But lately I'm falling short on the dealing and supplying end of things

The thought sends a chill down my spine, but at the same time a feeling of ease flows through me.

A knock at my door steals my attention and draws my eyes up.

"Who is it?" I ask loud enough for whoever it is to hear.

"It's me, boss," Tony says from the other side of the door.

"Come on in," I tell him.

My office door opens, and I push the picture frame away. He's seen it already. I'm not hiding it; I just don't like looking at Emma when I'm talking business.

Tony's got a stack of mail in his hands, one envelope already open. He tosses the envelopes on the desk in front of me and hands me the one that's open.

"Just some bills." I take the one he's opened and glance at

it. "I didn't know Ma wasn't takin' the chemo anymore." There's a bit of hurt in his voice, as if I kept it from him.

My body chills at his statement. "She's doing something different." He's always calls her Ma. Growing up next to each other, growing up so closely, she was his mother, too.

He grew up with his grandma, but she passed away a few years ago. She was never really there for him anyway. It wasn't her fault; she just wasn't ready to take care of a young kid when she was so old. His mom up and left though, leaving his grandma no choice.

"They're trying this new thing." I sigh, pinching the bridge of my nose and waving my hand in the air, trying to remember what they called the pills. "It's still chemo, just in pill form. They said it'll help without making her body so weak."

"Is it helping?" he asks.

"I don't know." It's a *cocktail*. Another one. Just a different mixture of the same shit. I shake my head, trying not to think about it. Ma's not looking any better. She says she's not feeling any better either.

"I was talking to her yesterday," Tony says casually. I know he's faking being relaxed though. He's not looking at me; instead he's looking out the window of the office. I know him well enough to know that he's got something he doesn't want to tell me. He's holding back.

"Oh yeah?" I ask.

He takes a seat in the chair across from me. His body's a little stiff, although he's trying not to show it. It's making me nervous. We share everything, and I don't know what the hell's going on with him right now.

"Yeah." His fingers tap nervously against the armrest as he clears his throat. "She was asking about the special stuff." The bastard has the nerve to look me in the eyes as he says that.

The special stuff. The shit that's meant to make death fast and easy. Given in their sleep.

It means she's asking for a way to die. My throat dries up instantly. I struggle to breathe, and I can't even swallow. It's not the first time she's done this. I look away and out the window.

A few weeks ago she was asking me for it. Not outright, but just hinting around about it. I couldn't take it. I don't want her to talk like that. And I couldn't let her do that to herself. I'm not letting her give up. She's going to beat this.

"You better be careful, Tony," I tell him slowly, finally facing him again. My voice is gruff. It almost cracks. I almost looked weak in front of him. I've never thought of him as an enemy, but right now, that's exactly what he looks like to me. He throws his hands up in defense. Again he has the nerve to look me in the eyes. "I'm just telling you what she said." He shakes his head somewhat, but there's a look in his eyes I don't trust. "I just wanted you to know."

"I know." My voice gets louder and I can't help it, but my emotions are taking over. I hold onto the anger more than anything else. That's the one I can handle.

I push back the sense of betrayal I feel over her for wanting to end it. For not trying. For being willing to leave me. I can't take it. My voice cracks this time, but I don't care as I say, "She's gonna fight this." My fist slams against the desk. "She's going to beat this." I feel unhinged, like a beast trapped in a cage, trying desperately to get out. Fighting just to live. Fighting for her to live.

"I hear you, Derek." His voice is shaky, and his eyes glass over. "You know she's my Ma, too." The only thing that saves him right now is that he's getting emotional. I stare at him for a long time without speaking, just breathing, trying to keep myself restrained. I hate that he even brought it up.

What's worse is I hate that it's true. I don't doubt him for a second. I'm sure she asked him for it.

"What'd you tell her?" I ask him.

"I told her I'd ask you." This time he doesn't look at me. He keeps his eyes trained on the pile of papers on my desk. His voice is low and full of pain. "She shouldn't have to live like this." I glare at him, willing him to look me in the eye, and give him a deadly look. "It's spreading." Although his voice is quiet, the words slam against me as though he screamed them.

"Shut up, Tony." I get out of my chair so fast that it rolls back and it hits the wall hard behind me. I tower over him and shout, "Get out!" I stare at him, willing him to leave before I lose my shit and beat the piss out of him.

He gets up without a word. The only sound in the room is the scraping of the chair legs against the wooden floor.

I'm breathing heavy as he opens the door and then slams it behind him.

I spend thousands of dollars a month. I'll spend thousands more. Whatever it takes, I'll pay them. That's worked for years. It's what fueled my desire to rise to the top. It's the only thing I've worked for. The only reason I took this path back then. I needed the cash. I needed to help her. She still needs me, but what else do I have to give her?

All the money in the world, and it can't save her.

What good is it? What good is any of it?

I grip the desk to keep myself standing upright, my chest heaving with each breath. My eyes fall on the picture. The one of me and Emma, in the frame Ma gave me. I instantly reach for my phone and call her.

I need my sweetheart. I need her to take this pain away.

CHAPTER 13

Emma

I've spent the last few days with Derek, as in barely leaving his sight; he only left this morning because he had to. Something's wrong, but he won't tell me what. I've seen his mom, and she isn't telling me anything either.

Other than my paranoia, things are falling back into place, just like when we were back in high school except it isn't a secret anymore. We spend most of our days tangled up together, but the same problems that ripped us apart are staring straight back at me. I don't want to fall for him only to wind up brokenhearted. I can't handle going through what I went through last time, because it will be so much worse this time.

I slowly walk down the stairs after taking a long, hot shower. I'm not in a rush to do anything.

The clinking of dishes tells me Sandra's in the kitchen.

I walk unhurriedly to her, my fingers trailing along the wall as I stare at the faded designs in the paisley runner that lines the hallway.

Sandra looks over her shoulder as I enter the kitchen. "Hey chica," she says with a smile and returns to the dirty dishes and suds.

"Hey," I say listlessly. I grab a bottle of water from the stainless steel fridge and sit down at the kitchen table in the corner, playing with the plastic cap. "What does Tony do?" I ask her.

"He's employed by Derek." She turns her head to talk while she's scrubbing a frying pan. "Technically it's Wade LLC. Or something like that. I'm not really sure." And with that, she turns back to the sink. As if knowing a company's name is all that matters.

"But what does he *do*?" I pry. I need to know if she knows about all of Derek's businesses. Specifically the one that's making me freak out. I try to take a sip of water, but I don't want it. I set it back down on the table and pick up the cap, rolling it between my fingers.

"I don't know. Do *you* know what he does?" she challenges. She drops the frying pan she just washed into the dish drainer a little harder than necessary. My eyes fly to hers.

"No," I say easily, not wanting to fight with her. "That's why I'm asking you." I start peeling the label off my water bottle, picking at the edges slowly. I don't want to piss Sandra off, but I don't know how she handles Tony dealing, and all the dangers that come with it. No matter what Derek says, I know it's not safe.

Sandra huffs out a deep breath. "He mostly works in the greenhouse. That's what he told me."

"And you believe him?" He's Derek's best friend. I can't believe that he only works in the greenhouse. I can't see a man like Tony watering plants and picking leaves or whatever the hell they do.

Her body tenses. She turns off the water and turns around to face me, picking up a dishtowel off the counter.

She's pissed off. "Yeah, of course I do. He wouldn't lie to me," she says as she dries her hands. She leans against the dark granite countertop, facing my direction.

I stare at my water bottle, rather than her. I can feel her watching me rip my water bottle label up. This isn't about her or Tony.

"I don't ask questions, Emma," she says after a long moment, breaking the silence.

"I just have to," I confess as I turn to look at her. I can feel the tears welling up in my eyes. I can't just pretend anymore.

She walks over to the kitchen table and sits down next to me. Her expression softens as she finally realizes I'm not here to fight with her over her decisions. She puts her hand on my shoulder and squeezes gently; it's a compassionate touch, and one that I needed. "Yeah, I did, too. But the thing is... he can't just walk away. And he's doing the best he can. The bad things... sometimes they happen. But I don't wanna hear about them. I don't wanna be a part of it. You know?" she tells me, her eyes wide and pleading.

"But don't you love him?" I don't understand how she can just turn a blind eye to what's going on.

"Of course I do," she says sincerely.

"Then I don't understand," I say, shaking my head.

Exasperated, she stands up and walks back to the sink. "Just don't ask questions, Emma."

I stare at her back as the sound of running water hits my ears, wondering how she does it. I don't think I can do it. I clean up the shredded label, throw it in the trash, and head back upstairs, my chest hurting and feeling more conflicted than I did before I approached her.

I fall onto my bed, burying my head into my pillow. What am I going to do? I'm falling for Derek. *Hard.* I knew I would. I was so stupid to do this. Stupid to get involved with him again.

It's going to rip me to shreds when this tears us apart. I lift my head up and stare at the grey and white area rug on top of the hardwood floor.

I don't see how it could end differently this time. Derek is still bad news. I need to focus on school and my career. I've worked so hard; I can't fuck it up now. I can't see a future with him, not with him doing this shit.

I want one though. God help me, I want a life with him. I wish I didn't know.

I swallow thickly and ignore how I'm feeling. When I leave the state and go back to school, I'm sure things will change. The distance will make it easier. That's what the real problem is. We're like magnets drawn to one another, needing each other's touch. We need space between us. The very thought makes me hate myself. But I can't lie to myself anymore. He's not good for me.

I grab my books from my Kate Spade bag that's lying on the dresser. Sitting cross-legged on the bed, my back leaning against the headboard, I decide to bury myself in work. That's all I'll have when he's gone anyway. The realization makes me feel so empty.

There are so many topics in this book that relate to him; children growing up with an abusive parent, children and teens turning to drugs to help them cope.

The back of my head bangs against the headboard.

I shove the book away and lie down. I put my hands over my eyes. They feel so cool. It's so comfortable. I turn lazily and grab the remote off the nightstand, turning on the TV. I just need to do something mindless. Turning onto my side, I put the throw pillow between my knees and cover up with the white crocheted blanket neatly folded at the end of the bed. I flick through the channels until I find the Lifetime Movie Network. There's some love story-turned-murder mystery on.

This is exactly what I need to do, just veg out and relax.

Halfway through the movie, my phone goes off. It shakes me out of a near-sleep state, and it's then that I hear Sandra in her room. I'm not sure what she's doing, but I stretch and let out a small yawn before leaning across the bed to grab my phone.

It's Derek.

"Hi," I answer the phone as if nothing's wrong. But my heart hurts. I feel like I'm betraying him. I pick at the crocheted blanket as he talks.

"Hi, sweetheart." His voice is gravelly; he sounds upset. My stomach twists into knots. Something's wrong. My mind immediately goes to his mom.

I sit up on the bed, concerned. My heart races in my chest. "Are you okay?"

He sighs before answering, "I'm having a rough day. I could really use a distraction." I clench my teeth and close my eyes. He always does this. He's not going to tell me shit. I ball the blanket in my hand and wait a moment.

When I don't respond, he adds, "I want you to come over."

I really should tell him no. I should start distancing myself from him. But I can't do that to him now.

He's not okay. He needs me. I throw the blanket off me and climb out of bed.

"I'll be there soon."

CHAPTER 14

Derek

I STARE at the TV screen in the living room. It's playing something mindless. The soft sounds of the background music fill the room. I'm not paying any attention though. I'm just waiting for Emma.

She should be here soon. I left work early. I can't get anything done thinking about what my Ma asked Tony about. My eyes focus on the hallway. Ma's bedroom door is open. She's reading her books, just like always. When I came home I had intended on asking her why she did it. Why she felt the need to go to him. Why she felt the need to give up.

But when I walked into her room, she had a sweet smile on her face. She was having a good day. She asked me to tell her something new, just like she always does.

I couldn't ruin the moment. I don't know how many I have left with her.

I know it's not okay. The way I handle things isn't

healthy. Emma's been telling me that so fucking much lately. I just try to forget my problems. At least the personal things. When it comes to work though, it's a different story. I take everything head on. But when it comes to this, when it comes to my mother?

I'd rather just pretend that everything's all right. It's so much easier, so much better than thinking it's all going to come to an end before I'm ready.

The sound of the front door opening draws my attention. Emma doesn't even knock anymore. It's only been a little over three weeks, but there's a sense of ease between us, an understanding. We both know what we feel for each other. We both know the type of people we are. But just like Ma, I refuse to think of the inevitable. Emma keeps bringing it up, telling me she's going to be leaving soon.

I don't want her to go back to school. It's coming way too soon. Things feel like they're on the edge of a cliff, ready to fall over and shatter. And she's not gonna be here.

I already know I'm a selfish man. Wanting to keep her here doesn't make me any different.

The door closes and I finally get up from my seat, hitting the button on the clicker to turn the TV off.

"Derek?" I hear Emma call out from down the hall. Her soft voice echoes off the walls. I'm sure Ma can hear it, too.

Emma's almost at Ma's room before I can even respond. It's become a habit for her, to check in on my mother. And to let her know she's here. She pauses just before the open door. I quicken my pace to meet her there.

The look on her face tells me she knows something is wrong. It's the "we gotta talk" look. I hate that expression. She always wants to talk.

I shake my head, not wanting to let her know what's going on. Part of me wants to open up to her about the tension between me and Tony, but I'm just not that kind of guy. I don't say a word, my jaw clenched, as I lead her into Ma's bedroom.

I splay my hand on her back and walk side by side with her over to Ma's bed. I wasn't planning on seeing Ma again tonight, but Emma would never let me hear the end of it if she didn't at least say hello. We've already been through this. And I'm a pushover when it comes to her.

I clear my throat and grab my chair that's still next to Ma's bed. I didn't put it back to where it goes in the corner earlier today; I guess some part of me knew I'd be back in here tonight. I pull Emma by the waist, letting her sit on my lap.

"You and those dirty books," Emma jokes with Ma.

"You know you like them too," my mother teases her back.

I have to laugh. "Ma, you know Emma doesn't read those books. She's too busy with school. She only has time to read books about ethics and stuff like that."

Emma's head whips around to me. "How do you know what I read?"

I look up at her with my brow furrowed. "I look at your books." Of course I know what she reads. I wanted to know what she was up to. I wanted to know what she spends all her time doing. Not that I'm interested in reading that kind of shit, but I'm interested in what she's interested in.

Ma pipes up, "I read an article that said women who read *these* kinds of books are smarter than the average woman." Emma huffs a small laugh with a sweet smile on her lips.

Ma looks straight at me. "I know your girl is smart, Derek. That's why I gave her a few of my favorites." Emma and Ma laugh, but I can't join in. I find myself just staring at Ma. It's a rare day when happiness is so evident on her face. She's showing it today. Like nothing's wrong with her other than the weight loss. Emma brings this out in her. I don't understand why Ma doesn't fight harder. She's been so happy, the happiest I can ever remember her being ever since Emma walked through that door. My chest pangs with sadness and guilt.

Maybe if I'd never let Emma walk away in the first place back then, maybe that would've made a difference.

I couldn't give Ma the happiness she needed while I was building this business and providing for her. But it's here now. Why has she given up now?

"I may have already read one. It only took me a few hours." Ma laughs and smacks her thigh at Emma's confession. The two of them go back and forth for a little while. I'm used to this now. They hit it off. Usually they're making fun of me. Until today, I enjoyed it. I looked forward to it, even.

But as I sit here watching the two of them, I can't even focus on what they're saying. It's like I'm watching in slow motion. All the sounds are muffled. I don't know what they're saying, but I know the way I feel. I know the way they're making each other feel.

That's what matters at the end of the day. That's what memories are really made of. Emotions.

I wish I had a camera now, not because I want to remember Ma looking like this. I don't. But I want to remember how happy she is right now.

"You all right?" It takes me a moment to realize Emma's question is directed at me.

I clear my throat. "Yeah, I think I just need some coffee. I've had a headache all day," I lie. I promised her that I wouldn't lie to her. I promised myself too, but in this moment, I need to do it.

"Time for you two to head out. You don't need me." Ma picks her book back up and says, "I'm just an old lady over here with her dirty books." She smiles. Although Ma is making it sound funny, just joking around like she usually does, it hurts me to hear her say that.

"I need ya, Ma." That's all I can say before I gently push Emma off my lap. She stands up easily, although she looks back at me with concern. As soon as her feet hit the ground, I'm up and out of the room. I can hear Emma as she follows me out of the room and down the hall. I feel like a little bitch as tears well up in my eyes, but I push them away. I'm not gonna cry. I'm gonna figure this out. There has to be a way. I go straight to the liquor cabinet in the kitchen. I need to chill the fuck out right now. Emma grabs my arm as the door to the whiskey flies open.

"Derek, what the hell's wrong?" Emma's eyes look straight into mine, pleading with me and flashing with worry. It makes me sick. All I've done is brought worry into her life. That's all I'm good for.

"Tell me!" she yells at me.

I can't lie to her even though I want to. I don't want to admit what my mother asked. Mostly because I don't want Emma's opinion. I swear to God if she says the same thing that Tony says, I'm not sure I'll be able to forgive her. For some reason, Tony gets away with it. Maybe because I know how much he loves her. But with Emma, it would break my heart if she told me to give in to what Ma wants. I don't think I could forgive her.

"She's not doing good." That's all I can get out now. The other words won't come. I'm all choked up. I move a couple steps over, ignoring the look on her face, ignoring the pleading of her eyes to tell her what's going on.

"Is she not responding to the new treatment?" Emma asks. Her and Ma talk a little about the treatments, but it's just small talk.

Emma doesn't know the details. She doesn't even know that Ma's technically on hospice. The doctors are just waiting for her to die. I had to keep fighting for this. I had to keep getting the medicine for her. I'm trying not to give up hope even when she does. I'm trying not to anyway, just desperately trying to hold on. But in the last few days, hope has been slipping away.

"It's not that," I say as I pour the whiskey into the short glass. If Emma wasn't here, I wouldn't even bother with it. I'd be drinking straight from the bottle.

"What is it?" she asks me. Her voice is so small, it's full of fear.

"I don't know what to do." I give her that much, but I can't tell her exactly what I'm talking about. I can't give that to her. I'm afraid that the more I give her, the more she'll see me and the reality of my life. The more she'll realize that she shouldn't be with me.

"You're smart, Sweetheart," I say and take a sip of my whiskey before looking at her. She's gripping the granite countertop tightly, looking at me like she's barely holding on for dear life. "Tell me what to do."

"You're smart, too," she says softly. She takes a small step closer to me, her hands rubbing soothing circles on my back. I know she means it to be comforting, but all I want to do is push her away right now. I don't want to be comforted. I realize I don't even want a distraction as I take another sip of the burning whiskey. I slam the glass down on the counter and almost shove her back, but I don't. I can't take this shit anymore.

But I can't risk losing her and having no one. Even though that's what I deserve.

"I can't figure out what to do," I tell Emma. "There's no way to win."

"Sometimes it's not up to you." Emma stares straight at me as she says the words.

I shake my head and insist, "You can always do something. There's always a choice. Even if you're making the wrong choice, it's up to you."

"You're wrong," she says and stops rubbing the soothing circles on my back. She shakes her head, saying, "Sometimes you don't get a say. Sometimes it's just the way life is."

In that moment I love her for her honesty, but I hate that she said it. I wish she'd just lied to me.

I close my eyes and reach for the whiskey, but her hand grips my wrist.

"Don't do this, Derek," she says with a strong voice. "You know she doesn't want to see you like this. This isn't the way to handle it."

"I don't want to see her like that!" I yell. My voice is harsh, and I instantly regret it. The look on Emma's face is like I slapped her. The room is quiet for a long time. I swirl the whiskey around in the glass and then bring it to my lips. I just want to get lost in the alcohol. "Tell me what to do then, Emma," I say in a low voice.

"First, you need to kiss me," she says in a shaky voice. "You need to know that no matter what happens, I'm still gonna be here." She takes the glass from my hand and dumps the whiskey down the sink, placing the glass on the countertop before looking back up at me. She pushes herself between the counter and my chest, her body touching mine.

I lower my head, putting my lips to hers as she cups my jaw. It's not a kiss like any other kiss we've had, not at first. But she doesn't let me go until I soften my lips. Until they mold to hers. My arms wrap around her small body. I hold onto her tightly as she kisses me back fiercely, refusing to let me go until I feel like I'm falling to pieces around her.

She finally pulls away from me, visibly swallowing, her eyes on my lips. She lays her head on my chest. "Some days are going to be hard." She takes a deep breath. "Some days you're not gonna know what to do. Some days you won't even remember."

I want to pull away from her at the last line, realizing what she's talking about. But she holds me tighter, and she keeps going without waiting for me to even acknowledge how fucked up that sounds. I don't wanna talk about what it's going to be like when Ma's gone.

"And when you realize you've forgotten, when you have a good moment and you realize that you weren't thinking about her, you might even hate yourself."

I suck in a breath; I hate thinking about this. I hate feeling like this.

"But she wants you to be happy, Derek." She looks up at me, her hazel eyes pleading with me. The green swirls and blue specks shine brightly over the glassy tears in her hazel eyes. "She wants you to have a life after she's gone."

I shake my head. "I'm not ready for that," I barely whisper, my voice breaking. "I promised her." I wipe the bastard tears from my eyes, sniffling and trying to pull away from her, but she doesn't let me. I don't want her to see me like this. I don't want to be the weak man I am right now. "I promised her when I was a kid that I'd make sure she'd be all right." I take an unsteady breath, calming myself slightly at the memory. Pops had just left. I knew Ma wasn't healthy, and the late nights at the diner were only draining the life from her faster. "I told her that she'd beat this. I promised her that she'd live to see a hundred."

Emma parts her lips, but doesn't say anything. Her eyes are filled with so much sadness. Her voice cracks as she says, "Some things are out of our control. You made a promise you can't keep."

I JOG down the stairs on my way out to go see Emma. I almost leave without saying bye to Ma. It's pretty late and I know she went down for a nap earlier, but I want to make sure I see her before I go. It's a good habit to be in, just so she knows where I am. I see her door's open as I walk toward it to stand in the doorway. My hands grip the molding on the outside, and I lean into the doorway slightly. "Hey, Ma." I still feel like shit from the other day. It's been a couple days since Emma was over and I could barely keep it together in front of Ma. She hasn't mentioned it or brought it up though. That's what Ma does, she never holds anything against me. It's what she's always done, and that's what I do, too.

She looks up at me, the thin-rimmed glasses on her face slipping down her nose slightly. She closes the thick romance novel in her hands and sets it beside her. "You going out?" I take a few steps into the room, and she keeps on going. "Are you going to go see Emma tonight?" Her brows are raised, and I almost blush from the look on her face.

"I was going to." I sag into the seat next to her bed.

"I think that girl is good for you, Derek," she says as she nods her head slightly.

"You just like her because she likes your dirty books, too." I nod at the book in her hands as I add, "She's supporting your habit," I joke. I never thought the two of them would have something like *that* in common.

"It makes me happy to see you so happy, Derek." Ma's voice is a little bit more serious. It catches me off guard.

I nod, looking at the thick comforter on Ma's bed. "She definitely makes me happy." Ma's pale blue eyes seem to get a little bit brighter as her expression softens. It's a look I don't remember ever seeing on her face. She clears her throat and brings the comforter up closer around her waist and picks her book back up. "You better go to her then," she murmurs as she opens her book and pushes her glasses back up her nose. "That girl loves you, Derek; I can see it." She doesn't look at me as she says the words. She peeks up at me without moving her head as I rise from the seat. "And you love her too, don't you?"

"Come on, Ma." I shoo away her question, tossing my hand in the air and walking toward the door.

"Do your mama a favor and be honest with me right now. It's something I need to know, Derek." The look on her face is completely serious, and again I don't anticipate it.

I think about it, really think about my feelings for Emma. But the truth is, I started loving her a long time ago, and I never stopped. This is nothing new; the love I have for her has been constant. It's only grown if anything. I grip the handle on the door and nod my head as I say, "Yeah, Ma. I think I love her."

Ma shakes her head slightly and says, "I know you do." She sits back in her bed, getting comfortable. "Could you go ahead and shut that door for me, baby?"

I've been so used to her leaving it open, I didn't think about closing it. "Yeah, love you, Ma." She gives me a soft smile as she says, "I know you do. And I love you, too. Don't you ever forget that."

CHAPTER 15

Emma

I'm going to miss this when I leave for school. That's all I can think as I lie under the comforter in Sandra's guest room with Derek. This moment feels right, it feels safe. But it's going to be gone before I know it.

Ever since he broke down and told me about his mom, things have been different. He's finally opening up to me instead of pushing me away. And I feel closer to him than ever before. I've fallen for him. Completely. I'm in love with Derek Wade. The thought makes me want to kiss him and run from him all at the same time. Either way, I'd be left breathless.

"What are you thinking?" he asks me.

He's running his fingers through my hair as I lie with my head on his chest. The sound of his heartbeat is steady and soothing. My fingers lazily trace circles on his bare chest. This moment is so close to being perfect.

"I'm just happy right now," I answer as I continue to caress his chest, moving down to his stomach. *Right now* being the words he won't register as important.

"Yeah? I'm feeling pretty happy right now, too. Thanks to you," he says and kisses the top of my head.

I lick my lips and try to get rid of the sick feeling in the pit of my stomach.

"I can't believe my break is almost over. I'm not looking forward to going back next week," I admit. I'm dreading being so far apart from Derek, especially with how sick his mom is. He pulls me closer, resting both hands on my hip. I can't believe how much has happened in the past four weeks. I don't want this to end. If only you could pause time and live in a single moment forever.

"I'm not going to like you being so far away, but it's only for a few months. And I'll definitely be coming down to see you," he says as he runs his hand down my back. "We'll make this work. Don't worry, sweetheart." He kisses my hair and runs his hand up and down my arm as he says, "You know I can't stay away from you for long."

I pick my head up off his sculpted chest to kiss him.

My body reacts the moment our lips touch. We've spent most of the day in bed, and I still want more. I'm not sure I'll ever get enough of him. Thank God Sandra and Tony are at Tony's for the weekend.

He slowly kisses down my jaw to my neck. He's already hard again, I can feel him pressing insistently against my hip. As I go to climb on top of him, his phone rings.

A chill sweeps through my body, killing the mood. Who would be calling him so late?

He doesn't make a move to go for it. "Do you need to get that?"

"No, it's not important," he says as he continues kissing down my neck.

"But what if it's someone from *work*?" I ask as I slide off him, ignoring how his hands at my hip are trying to hold me to him.

He strokes my cheek softly. "It doesn't matter, sweetheart. When I'm with you, I'm with you. No one else matters." He pulls me on top of him and starts kissing my collarbone, running his hand down my back to my ass.

His phone starts ringing again. The hairs on the back of my neck stand up, and I have a bad feeling about this. "Are you sure?" I ask, glancing at his phone and then back at him.

I know his mom has a different ringtone, so it's not her. It's not his house calling, but I don't like it. I have a really bad fucking feeling.

"I'm positive. Come on, it's late. Let's get some sleep," he says and he pulls me closer to him. He covers us both with the down comforter, and wraps his arm around my waist.

I hope it isn't anything important and that it's just my paranoia. I try focusing on his steady heartbeat and rhythmic breathing.

But a moment later it goes off again. I push off of him and give him a look.

He sighs with exasperation and crawls out of bed, walking over to the dresser to check his phone, the third call going to voicemail before he's able to answer.

He puts his phone to his ear to listen to his voicemail. I pull my knees up to my chest as I wait for him to tell me everything is okay and that he was right. But my heart stills in my chest as his expression changes.

The blood drains from his face. It's bad. Whatever's happened is bad. Fuck. My heart squeezes into a painful knot.

"I have to go," he says, pulling his jeans on and stepping into his shoes.

I'm already out of bed, grabbing a pair of yoga pants off

the floor and trying to put them on quickly. "What is it, what's wrong?"

"It's my Ma, I have to go. I'll call you later," he says, turning toward the door.

Pulling a hoodie over my head and not bothering with a bra, I yell, "Derek! Wait! Is she okay? I'll come with you!"

"I'll be fine. Just stay here. I'll call you later," he says shortly. Goosebumps prick over every inch of my skin at his rejection. Is he really pushing me away right now? He knows I know how close he and his mom are. If she's not okay, I want to be there.

"Let me come with you. Let me be there for you," I beg him while grabbing a pair of socks.

"Emma, I don't fucking have time for this! Stay here. I'll talk to you later," he yells as he storms out of the room. I can't believe him. I know he's hurting right now, but he can't just push me away like this. He knows as well as I do that he needs someone. I need someone too.

He's not emotionally stable right now; he's not going to be able to handle this. He's hurting, and he needs someone. Everything in me is telling me that he's going to need me. I run after him, banging the door against the wall and chasing him down the stairs.

The front door slams before I'm able to get to him. I stare at it, my mouth open and lungs barely functioning.

After a moment, my body starts trembling. I always listen to him. I never tell him no. And that's my fault. It's going to ruin me. But listening to him right now is going to ruin *us*. I can't let it happen. I know it with everything in me.

I head back upstairs to put my sneakers on. I'm not going to listen to him this time. Fuck that. Something's wrong, and he needs me.

I grab my phone to text Sandra to see if she knows what's

going on. Hopefully, Tony told her about whatever's going on with his mom.

I slow my steps, my heart pausing. His mom. I shake my head, my throat closing as I think about seeing her yesterday. No, she's going to be okay. I swallow the spiked lump that's suffocating me and ignore it. Brushing the tears from my eyes I throw my hair up into a bun, grab my wristlet and my keys then head downstairs.

I'm checking my phone what seems like every thirty seconds. For Sandra, for Derek. I just want to know what's going on. I stifle the emotions threatening to cripple me. I focus on my breathing and on Derek snapping at me like that.

The anger comes back and it's easy for me to ignore the pain.

I can't believe he expects me to just sit back and let him handle this on his own. He can't just push me aside and take on something like this alone.

I climb in my car, the freezing cold sending a chill down my spine, turning my breath to fog in front of my face, and my phone dings. Sandra finally texted me back. I turn the key, bringing my car to life before checking her text.

My mouth goes dry and my heart stops when I read her message, my entire body feeling like ice; Derek's mom died.

CHAPTER 16

Derek

My eyes fucking hurt from crying. I wish I could make it stop, but I can't. She can't be gone. I just saw her this morning. I just talked to her before I went to Emma's.

I press my palms to my eyes, hating the bitch tears.

I knew she was going to leave me soon, but I didn't want to believe it. Nothing could prepare me for this. There's an emptiness inside my chest that I don't think will ever be filled. And if it is, I don't want to live to see that day.

Tony's in the corner of the room with red-rimmed eyes. His nose is red, too. He has a box of tissues that's half gone. The rest are crumpled up in the trashcan.

It's just the two of us; Ma's not here anymore.

They pronounced her dead and took her away. They said she died in her sleep.

I stand up and walk to the window of the dining room, looking out at the snow. It's going to be cold when we bury her. I guess that's the way it should be.

I take in a ragged breath. Emma's been helping me. She's been preparing me. It's different for her since it's not her mother. But she has a softness about her. A way that she eases reason into me. I didn't want to let go of Ma.

But I knew it was coming. Everyone knew what was coming. I wish I could've fought it for her. I wish I could've traded places with her. My heart clenches in my chest and another sob threatens to go through me, but I shut it down.

The cops and ambulance just left. It's funny how people look at you when your mother's gone. No one's looked at me like that since high school. Maybe even since before then. Maybe since middle school when I'd show up with bruises on my arms from when Pops used to beat me. Maybe it's really been that long since someone has looked at me with such sympathy in their eyes.

I can't take it.

I don't want to see that look in Emma's eyes. I don't want her here. I don't want her to see me like this. There's an anger brewing inside me, threatening to come out. What's worse is that I want it. I want to unleash. I don't want to feel anything but that rage. It'd be so much better than feeling everything else. If I could feel nothing, I'd much rather that. But I'll settle on the anger for now.

"She begged me." Tony's words pull my focus from the snow falling outside and bring me back to him. I turn to look at him, trying to make sense of what he just said. He's not looking at me. He's hunched forward in his seat. He's still crying. He's still fucked up.

"She knew you wouldn't," he says in a jagged voice. His words slowly hit me. I stand still next to the cold window. The air has a hint of the freezing chill that gently blows against my skin. It keeps me frozen in place as I watch him.

"She could feel herself slipping. She didn't want you to see her like that. She was ready."

"What the fuck are you talking about?" I ask him, feeling breathless and lightheaded. It's like I'm not really here. Like I'm just watching this scene unfold.

"She didn't want me to tell you. But I can't hide it from you."

No. My head's shaking on its own, denying what he's telling me.

"She asked for the shot, and I gave it to her. I waited until she was asleep. I'm sorry, Derek," his voice cracks as he wipes the tears from under his eyes.

He continues to cry, looking up at me, waiting for my reaction. Waiting for my forgiveness, maybe? For understanding?

I stare at him, looking so dejected in that chair. Letting the words sink into every vein. Letting them flow through my blood.

My body moves before I'm conscious of it. My boots smack against the floor as my hand balls into a fist. My knuckles crack against his jaw before I even know what's going on.

He falls to the floor without even trying to defend himself, but that doesn't keep me from getting on top of him. My hand wraps around his throat, but I'm not fast enough. His fist slams against my nose, cracking against bone. The pain radiates to my temples, and the metallic taste of blood fills my mouth.

It hardly affects me. The disbelief of what he's done, the betrayal of what he's telling me, is all-consuming. Rage burns deep inside of me.

I don't waste any time slamming my fist into him again, planting a hard blow against his high cheekbone. He's just as quick. His legs grip my waist, wrapping around me and pushing me down to the ground as he rolls over. He tries to pin my hands down to keep me from knocking the shit out of him, but I'm too strong for him.

I elbow the fucker in the face as he tries to tell me to calm down. I can hardly hear the words he's screaming at me. Only white noise is ringing loudly in my ears. Blinding white light flashes before my eyes, and then it all turns red. My knuckles scream with pain over and over and over as they slam into his face. He's holding on, taking each blow. He's fighting me back though.

I pour all of my emotion into each hit. I try to move my legs up to get a grip on him, but his thighs are holding me down, pinning me to the floor. He can't get a grip on my wrists though; he's trying, but all it's doing is giving me access to his face. I continue the punches, one after the other. My knuckles split from the impact, the pain shooting through me.

"You bastard!" I scream, finally finding my voice. I yell so loud it hurts, the words scraping against my throat as they leave me. I cling to the anger giving me so much strength; the full realization of what he said is hitting me so hard that I feel like I can't hold on. "You killed her!" I yell. I can't take it.

I struggle against him, and get away from his hold for just a moment. It's long enough for me to pound my fist into his shoulder. I want his throat though. I want to kill him. "I can't fucking believe you!" I don't know how I'm even capable of speaking. The words are flying out of my mouth without my conscious consent. My fist slams against Tony's jaw again. This time I hear bone crunch.

He took her away from me. I'll make him pay. He deserves to die.

"She wasn't okay!" he screams back at me. "She couldn't live like that!" I ignore everything that he screams at me. Every word uttered from his lips is the word of a liar, of a murderer. Not that I didn't already know that, because we've killed plenty, but my Ma is different. It's unforgivable.

His face is so close to mine. The heat is overwhelming. My body's shaking. Adrenaline is coursing so fast through my blood. It feels as if I can't control myself. As he grabs my left wrist, pinning it down, I smash my right fist into his throat. His hands instinctively reach for his neck, finally letting me up. I push him off of me, shoving my fist into his chest. He falls backward, landing hard on the ground. I'm quick to move and slam my knee into his thigh, pinning his body down and preventing him from getting away. I go for his throat with both hands, squeezing as hard as I can, and he goes for mine.

I struggle to breathe. His hands push into the soft spot just below my Adam's apple. His nails scrape and cut the back of my neck as he chokes me.

His face turns a bright red, swelling from the pressure I'm putting against his own throat, from the lack of oxygen. My body screams to let go of him. It begs me to try to pry his hands off of my throat. But I'd rather die than give up. I want to see the life drained from him. My heart clenches in my chest, pain radiating through every part of me. My body tingles with heated anger. Why him? Why'd he have to do it? Tony is the only friend I've ever had.

"I hate you." I can't get the words out. I can't get them all out. But I got out what matters. Sadness flashes in his eyes as he hears my words, and a sick part of me actually feels pain for him. A part of me wants to forget this happened. Another part of me wishes he'd never told me. *Why won't the world just lie to me?*

My lungs feel so empty. My head feels so light. The force of my hold on him slowly wanes as strength leaves me, my body shaking with a need to let go, the need to free myself from the force choking the life out of me.

"Derek!" I hear Sandra scream as she runs toward us.

"Get off him!" Sandra wails as she runs to us. A vision of her blurs as her fist slams against my face, whipping my neck to the side. Her nails scratch at my fingers, desperate to pull them away from Tony's throat.

"Stop it!" Her high-pitched screech nearly burst my eardrums.

She pushes all of her weight onto my chest, pushing Tony away from me and out of my reach. She struggles for a moment. But I have nothing left in me. He falls backward, away from me and out of my hold. My lungs heave in a breath at the first chance. I roll onto my side, coughing and struggling for air. My eyes burn, my body trembles.

After a few moments, I try to pick myself up. I look up at Tony. The man I grew up with. My best friend. The man who murdered my mother.

"I'll never forgive you for this," I tell him in a raspy voice, the moment I have the breath.

The hurt that was in his eyes earlier isn't there now. It's been completely replaced with anger. "I knew you wouldn't forgive me." His confession surprises me.

He holds my gaze as he says, "It wasn't about me and you. It was about her."

CHAPTER 17

Emma

I feel like the drive to Derek's is taking forever. My hands twist on the steering wheel as I steady my breath. I just want to be there to hold him. I wipe my eyes again as I turn onto his street, my chest feeling tight. I really need to pull myself together and be strong for him, but I keep thinking about her. His mom was such a sweet woman. My heart aches for him… and for me. I had to pull over to get out the tears, but they keep coming back. I thought I was prepared, but I think I was only preparing him.

I struggle to breathe in as I stop at the last red light. I swear I've hit everyone. I sit back in the seat. The intersection is devoid of anyone. Just darkness this late at night.

I wish Derek hadn't pushed me away. I don't think I'll be able to take it if he tells me to leave when I get there. I hit the gas slowly as the light turns green. I won't be able to take it. I want to comfort him and be there for him, but I'm not okay either. I need someone too.

I pull into Derek's driveway, the car only just now

starting to heat up. My body is trembling from a mix of the cold and my nerves.

I practically run up the stone path to the front door, but when I get there I pause. *Please don't push me away Derek. Please. I need you too.* It's unlocked, so I go right in. I don't even hesitate. My breathing comes in heavy, my lungs hurting from the sharp cold air.

I run down the hallway and straight for his mom's room. My heart's beating so fast; I'm still wishing it's not true. I still expect to find her there. It's foolish, but I can't help denying the truth of the simple text message.

But she's not there. Neither is Derek.

Her bed's empty, and the medical equipment is turned off. It's so quiet, so surreal. She was just in here, talking to me like nothing was wrong. I close my eyes remembering how she told me to take care of him. I didn't think much of it, but as I hear her voice I can see she was saying good bye. The last words she told me. I cover my mouth and hold in the sob as I lean against the wall. *I will. I promise I will.*

A moment passes, my body heating with the agony of her loss as I struggle to right myself.

I'm a fucking mess, but I'll be there for him. That's all I need to do. I take one last look around the blush-colored bedroom and walk back into the hall. I can't close the door. Something in me just wants to leave it open. I can't shut it.

I look over my shoulder for one final glance into the room as I walk away and down the hall. I almost call out for Derek, but then I hear a sound in the living room. I can't place what the noise is. But it draws me to him. A moth to flame.

It's so quiet. It's ominous. I walk into the dark room and whisper his name. He's sitting in the dark. I can just barely make him out. He's leaning forward in the white armchair with his head in his hands.

My heart breaks for him. I don't wait for him to look up; I go straight to him and wrap my arms tightly around him. He doesn't even say anything as he wraps his arms around my waist and buries his face in my shoulder.

I hold him for a long time, running my hands up and down his back and kissing the top of his head. His face is wet. He's obviously been crying. I can't take it. I don't want to ever see him in pain like this.

"It's okay," I whisper without thinking. It's not really. And I can't make it okay. I wish I could take it back. If only words were a physical thing, and I could rip them from the air before they reached his ears. My heart clenches in my chest as he shakes his head slightly, not responding.

"Thank you," he says after a few minutes. His voice is raw.

He quickly wipes around his eyes before picking his head up to look at me. My heart stops in my chest. Holy fuck! His left eye is almost swollen shut. My breath comes up short, and I don't know how to react.

What the fuck happened?

"For not listening to me. For coming," he says before leaning in for a quick kiss. He doesn't address the fact that it looks like he got hit by a fucking tractor-trailer of fists. There's a huge scratch down his neck, and several bruises forming on his jaw and cheek.

He got fucked up.

I can taste the salt from his tears on his lips. It takes me a moment to even register what he said.

I rub the back of his neck as I say, "Of course I'm here. I'm always going to be here for you." I say truthful words, but I'm still waiting for him to tell me why the hell he looks like that. I was only behind him by maybe a half an hour. I know I drive slower than him, and I had to take some time to process it when Sandra texted me. I was an emotional wreck, but I wasn't that far behind him. What the fuck happened?

"Ma…" Derek swallows thickly.

"I know," I say quickly, so he doesn't have to. "I texted Sandra after you left."

He nods his head once and then looks down, avoiding my gaze.

"You really are the sweetest person I have ever met," he says in a hoarse voice leaning into me again, his hold on me stronger than ever before.

I want to ask him about his face. The only thing I can think of is that he did it to himself. The thought makes me sick. I can't stand it. I need to ask him, but I can't right now. I'm struggling to process everything.

"Come on, why don't we have a drink and then try to get some sleep?" And with that, I pull him into the kitchen, my heart beating frantically as I try to figure out what happened.

He sits down on a stool at the island and runs his hands through his hair. "I don't even know where to begin with everything that I have to do this week. Ma's had everything in order for a while now, but I just can't think about making arrangements for her funeral." His voice cracks.

I grab each of us a glass from the cabinet, and pour some brandy in each. I need a drink, too.

"I'll help you. Don't worry about it tonight," I say as I carry the two glasses over to the island. As I set the glasses down, I see that his knuckles are bloody again. They're much worse than the night at the restaurant. I'm really hoping he just hit a wall though and not a person this time. I stare at them for a long moment, refusing to look at his face.

He notices, but doesn't say anything. Just like he always does.

We drink our brandy in silence. I'm waiting. I'll wait for him this time. He has to tell me. I won't pry. He has to know by now I won't judge him, that I only want to help him. And he needs help. He desperately needs help.

I grab his hands and look into his pale blue eyes. "I'm here for you," I tell him soothingly. I try to rub my thumb over his knuckles, but they hit the cuts and it stops me; it makes me pull away from him.

He looks down at the countertop as he says, "Don't leave me tonight, sweetheart. I need you. I don't want to be alone right now."

"I'm here, and I'll be here for as long as you want me," I say reassuringly. He looks so tired; he looks emotionally abused and raw. I want to hold him, scream at him to find out what he's done, and question him until he tells me the truth. But I can't.

He leads me toward the stairs, and I feel like shit. Nothing feels right. How can he just avoid something so obviously wrong? Even worse, how can I let him? *Because his mother just died!*

God, I feel sick.

As we get to the staircase, my phone goes off. It's Sandra. I anticipated she'd call me. I wonder what she would do about Derek. About finding him like this.

What the hell happened?

I respond back quickly, only pausing for a second.

What?

Her response is instantaneous.

Why did Derek attack Tony?

What the fuck!? My feet turn to stone, refusing to move as the message hits me. *Derek attacked Tony?* My heart stops in my chest as Derek tries to pull me along and up the stairs. I let him. I silence my phone, and I just try to breathe.

I can't believe he hit Tony. I eye him as we walk. What did he say? What did he do?

He keeps covering his face with his other hand. He needs so much help. He's so lost. I have no fear for my own life whatsoever, but for his? I'm so scared for him. My heart is breaking.

I stop at the entrance to his bedroom, and he keeps walking, right into the bathroom and washes his hands and splashes some water on his face.

I can't explain how I feel as I sit on the end of the bed. It groans slightly as I shift my weight.

I love a man who's fucked up. I know that. But I never guessed he'd take it out on Tony. I stare at the open door to the bathroom, wondering why.

Finally, I decide I have to ask him about it. I can't just pretend. Even with his mom dying. This is just too much. "Derek, what happened with Tony? Sandra just texted me," I say, trying not to sound accusing, as he turns off the faucet.

His jaw tenses, and he clenches his fists. Anger and hatred are apparent on his face.

"He's dead to me," he says brusquely. I sit there in disbelief. My lips part, but I can't think of a response.

He climbs into bed, ignoring me. He lays down, but I can't. I won't. I wait a moment, trying to collect my thoughts and shift on the bed to be closer to him.

"I need you to tell me." I say quietly, the somber tone reflecting the air surrounding us.

"I can't," he says and then rolls onto his side, away from me. I suck in a sharp breath.

"You're not okay-"

"I know!" he yells. "Please, just drop it." He almost whispers the last part.

My shoulders tremble as I struggle with right and wrong, giving and taking. His mother just passed. He's physically and emotionally fucked up. I need to be here for him, but how can I be if he won't tell me what's going on in his head?

I go into the bathroom quietly and shut the door. I text Sandra back.

Derek won't tell *me anything. I didn't even know he attacked Tony until I got your text. WTF happened?*

I start pacing back and forth across the marble floor. It's a few minutes before I get her response.

Tony & *I were together at his place. Work called asked me to come in to help fix a mistake. T wanted to go see D's mom. Dropped him off on my way. 2hours later Tony messaged about D's mom. I pull up and hear shouting, go in. D was beating the shit out of Tony.*

Another text comes through as I'm reading the first one again.

Tried to pull them apart. *D said he'd never forgive T. T said it was about D's mom. He won't tell me anything.*

BURNED PROMISES

ALL I CAN KEEP thinking is What. The. Fuck? I sit down on the edge of the tub, gripping the cold porcelain edge.

I put my phone back in my wristlet, turn off the bathroom light, and open the door to the bedroom. Derek doesn't move when I walk into the room and set my wristlet on his dresser causing the metal chain to clink.

"I found out about your mom from Sandra," I say as I crawl into bed. "I found out about the fight from her too," my words are soft as I cuddle up to him. His stiff and unmoving, ready to push me away I'm sure. Refusing to open up. "I want to be here for you, but I need to know what's going on so I can give you what you need." I stare at his eyes, willing him to look at me, but he's focused on the ceiling, as if all the answers are written up there.

I rest my head on his forearm, his body's warm and inviting. He slowly wraps his arm around me, maybe realizing I don't want to fight. I'm just telling him the truth.

"Right now I just need you to lay with me. Just don't leave me." My throat feels like it's closing listening to the raw vulnerability in his cracked voice. I nod my head and kiss his shoulder before nestling down next to him.

I think sometimes you have to push people; sometimes you have to make them open up to you.

And other times you need to trust them. You just need to hold them.

Maybe I've been doing it all wrong all these years not pushing him, but in this moment, he just needs me to hold him. He needs *someone*.

I slip my shoes off and climb into bed next to him. I turn off the second table lamp and roll toward Derek. Kissing his shoulder, I wrap my arm around him.

Right now he just needs to feel loved. I can give him that, because I really do love him. Even if he is a broken mess.

I scoot a little closer to him, my eyes adjust to the dim

light of the night and I can see the dark bruise on his jaw. "Does it hurt?" I ask him softly.

He immediately nods his head, his forehead pinched and his breathing paused. "It hurts so much." His words are choked as he moves his hand over his face.

My heart splits into a thousand pieces as he breaks down in front of me.

"I'm here," I tell him with as much comfort as I can put in my voice. I try to hold him, but he doesn't move. I don't know what to do.

As if reading my mind, Derek says, "I'll be whatever you want. I'll give you whatever you want. I'll tell you everything. Please, just don't leave me." He finally opens his eyes, their filled with sadness and vulnerability, pleading with me.

"I promise I won't. I promise you."

How can I? When you love someone, they never leave you.

CHAPTER 18

Derek

It just started snowing. The sky is so thick with it that it's a greyish white. I hear someone cough from across the plot. My eyes travel to them for a moment, before focusing back down at the ground. The dirt looks loose, like it's just been placed.

My breath turns to fog in front of my face, and I know my nose and cheeks are a bright red from the cold. But I don't wanna leave yet. All I've been doing is looking at the flowers I've placed atop her grave over and over again. But leaving here… it feels like I'm leaving Ma.

I can't do it.

I need a break from this town. I severed every tie I have to it, except for the restaurants. I'm done with everything else. I gave the pot business to Tony. Left the all that shit on my desk for him and I know he got them. He made that clear in the emails he sent. I don't want a damn thing to do with it anymore. He can have it.

He's been texting me, calling me. He even showed up at the house a few times.

I called the cops the last time, and that was the only thing that got him to leave.

I don't wanna hear it.

I don't want to hear how he loved her.

How I was the one in the wrong for leaving her in pain when she was ready. He only said that once, but out of everything he said, that's what stuck with me. Cause that really hurt. *The truth always hurts the most.*

I still feel guilty about keeping it from Emma for as long as I did. But she broke me down. I confessed everything to her. She didn't run away like I thought she would. I made her promise she wouldn't, but I know promises don't mean shit sometimes. I want to give up on myself, but she won't let me. She's never broken a promise to me. And I'm starting to believe she'll really stay. I fucking hope she does. Without her, I don't know who I am anymore.

I thought the moment I told her what happened with Tony, that would be it for me, but she's still here. And I'm ready to move on from this shit life. I'm ready for something more. Something with her. I want to be the man she deserves. And I will. I'm walking away from all this shit.

"I don't wanna stay here." I finally speak, not able to keep thinking on the shit that's going through my head right now.

Emma's wrapped up tight in a thick, hooded black coat with a scarf around her neck. The tip of her nose is peeking out. She looks up at me, blowing hot air into her hands and then holding back onto my arm.

"We can go whenever you want," she says softly. I've been coming here every day for the last three days. So has Emma. She's missed the first few days of school, but she's not willing to leave yet. She hasn't left my side. If that's not true love, I don't know what is. I know with everything in me that I can't let her go.

"That's not what I mean," I tell her as I turn to face her. I wrap my arms around her waist as the light dusting of snow falls into her dark brunette hair. She's so fucking beautiful. She's more than a sweetheart. She's everything to me. "I wanna go with you."

"You wanna go to school?" she asks with disbelief.

A humorless laugh leaves me, and I look behind her before finding her eyes again. I don't need school. I've got more money than I'll ever need.

"Nah. Just go with you. I know you need to get back."

Her features soften as she realizes what I'm saying.

"I wanna be with you, Emma. I'm not letting you go this time."

She smiles softly and leans into me. "Come with me," she says softly. "I need someone, too."

I don't wanna leave Ma, but I can't stay here.

I give her one last kiss and start leading her to the car, walking through the graveyard and not looking back.

CHAPTER 19

Emma

WE JUST GOT to my tiny apartment, and it's strange seeing Derek here. He looks so at odds among all my cozy, chic accessories. I watch him as he picks up the small bird candelabrum in his hand. It's cast iron, and heavy. He holds it up and stares at it for a moment, then his brow furrows before setting it back down.

He takes in every item of the room slowly, processing this new environment. It's almost comical. His broad shoulders and tall stature seems out of place in my living room. My chairs are so tiny, I'm not sure how he'll even fit on them. I have a small IKEA sofa, and if he lay down on it, his legs would be hanging off the end.

He's picked up every picture frame I have on the shelf above my couch to look closely at each picture. He doesn't seem to know what to do with himself. He looks so lost.

BURNED PROMISES

I wish I already had a place for him here, but I don't. I will though. We'll make it work.

"We can go shopping," I offer. We're definitely going to need to go shopping. I forgot how girly and small my apartment is. He'll really freak out when he sees the bedroom. I still have the small single mattress from when I was growing up. Not that I wanted to keep it. I had to make a choice in what I could spend my money on. I decided that a queen mattress wasn't worth having over actual kitchen utensils and a dining room table to eat at. Besides, I'm petite.

"Yeah, I think we should definitely go out today," he says. The look on his face makes a small laugh come from my lips. I cover my mouth, feeling the blush rise to my cheeks. He smirks at me, shaking his head.

"I'm sorry, I just never thought I'd see you here."

"Did you really think it was over between us?" he asks, walking toward me. The way his hips are moving and his eyes are piercing into me make him seem like a lion hunting his prey.

I try to breathe, but it's hard with him looking at me like that. Like he wants me. Like I'm his to take.

And I am.

"I never know what to think when it comes to you, Derek," I say. That's the truth, and I'm not sure that'll ever change.

We drove down together this morning. I still can't believe he wanted to come back to school with me.

He's giving up everything and starting over. No drugs. No secrets. I'm his and he's mine and together we'll get through this. I know we will.

He lets out a small laugh, but it doesn't seem real. "It's a nice place you got here, Sweetheart." He looks past me, at the kitchen. "You definitely put your touch on this place."

"And you haven't even seen the rest of it," I say sarcastically. My apartment is about as big as his living room was. He's definitely downsizing.

"Want to go get something to eat? I'm starving," I say to him while grabbing my keys off the hook by the door. Eat, shop. We'll take each day at a time. Just get through each one. It's difficult for him sometimes. But just one step at a time is all we need.

He puts down the stack of papers he was looking at, and stands up from the stool he was sitting on at the kitchen counter.

"Are these all of the places you're planning on applying to once you graduate?" he asks me.

I forgot I was looking through some of my options before I left to go to Sandra's for winter break. I stare at the one on top, I put them in order of most desirable.

"Yeah, they're the schools and offices I'm interested in. I don't know if I'll get a job at any of them, but we'll see." I shrug. "Are you hungry?"

"I can eat," he says, taking one last look around.

I TAKE him to one of my favorite places. It's just a small family-owned restaurant where they know me by name. It's nothing like the bistro Derek took me to. Here all the booths are covered with a tough red fabric. I don't even know what kind of fabric it is, but it's wipeable and that's what matters. Kay's Tavern is one of my favorites though. I love their hot wings. "You gotta order them extra crispy though," I tell Derek as the hostess walks us to a booth near the front window. It's a bay window, and lining it are a few large picture frames with magazine cutouts and newspaper articles inside of them from when they first opened. They won a few awards, too. I was telling him all about it on the drive over, but every bit of conversation only made me more and more anxious. I know that we've led separate lives until now, and that our past lives didn't mesh. It's a cold hard truth that I eventually accepted. But now he wants to try to blend into mine, and I don't know how that's going to happen.

The late evening sun makes the untouched snow out front look even prettier. But beyond that, the cars have driven over the snow and ruined the purity of the scene, leaving dirty slush in their wake.

That's just the way it is though. The pretty parts never last.

Across the street are rows of houses lining the busy road. In front of one of them are a couple of kids making snowmen. It makes me smile. Derek follows my gaze, and it makes him smile, too.

I watch him look around the old restaurant. Family pictures decorate the pale yellow walls. Wooden tables and chairs fill the room except for the row of booths that line the front windows.

An older lady with short, curly red hair walks toward our table. "Well hello, Miss Emma. We've been wondering when you'd be back from break," she says with a smile and a bit of her Philly accent. Kay is a funny lady. She's got a few kids at the university I go to. Running this place means long days and short nights for her, but it's paid her children's ways through college. She likes to joke that they better put her in a nice nursing home when she gets older.

"Hi, Kay. It's good to be back. This is..." I trail off as I'm not sure how to introduce Derek. We haven't really had *that* talk yet. We're together, but do I say he's my boyfriend? That sounds so lame. Do I say he's my friend?

"I'm her boyfriend, Derek. It's very nice to meet you, Kay," he says as he shakes Kay's hand and smiles.

"Well, it's nice to meet you too, Derek," Kay says as she

smiles at me. "He's a handsome one, Emma. Good for you." The way Kay lowers her voice and looks away with a blush makes my eyes widen. This is a side of Kay I haven't seen before.

I'm smiling from ear to ear, and it takes me a moment to realize what Derek just said. He's my boyfriend. It seems too childish for me to get all wound up over it. I pick up my water and hold the straw as I take a sip. *Derek Wade is my boyfriend.* The thought makes me want to laugh. He's so much more than a boyfriend, but I still like hearing the word. I like having a label on us, even if it does seem immature.

"Yes he is, very handsome," I say to Kay. "Derek, Kay is the owner of this restaurant."

"Oh, really?" he says. "Well, you've got a very nice place here. And you seem to do a great business."

"We do. Thank God," Kay says, looking around her restaurant. "What can I get you two tonight?" she asks as she pulls out her notepad.

"Can we have two of my favorite, Kay?" I ask with a smile.

"Of course, baby girl. I'll get that right in for you," Kay says as she scribbles our order down on the pad and then puts it back into her apron.

"What's your favorite?" Derek asks with a cocked brow.

"You'll just have to wait and see," I say with a small smile.

Derek's phone goes off, and my eyes glance down to the table where the sound is coming from, but he doesn't look at it. He's been ignoring his phone, ignoring everything really since we've gotten here. It makes me sad to think that he's just turning his back on his entire life, but at the same time, some of it's needed. There's nothing there for him back home. He has his businesses which he can run without really being there for right now anyway. That's the good part about being a silent partner. He's available online, and if we need to go back he can be there within a few hours. Right now he's on vacation. Supposedly.

"This is a pretty nice area," he says absentmindedly. "Are the places you're interested in working at close by?"

"Pretty close, within fifteen miles," I answer him. I start picking at the napkin in my lap. It's paper, and shreds easily.

"I love this area." I shrug as I talk, making it seem like it's not a big deal. But this conversation is something that needs to happen. There are a lot of low-income areas around here, and the city has a really hard time finding teachers and counselors who last in these school districts. I want to make a commitment to be here and help these kids. That's why I'm doing this, and why I got into this line of work.

"So that was a big factor in deciding where I wanted to apply," I tell him, as I take another sip of water. I look over to my right, waiting to see if Kay has our orders coming up soon or not. I know we need to talk about these things, but so much has happened so quickly. I'm nervous that he's just not gonna want to stay here with me.

"It looks like a place I could get used to," he says as he taps his fingers on the table.

"Really?" I ask, hopefully.

"It could be. I'd have to look into it a little more," he says easily, taking me by surprise. I just assumed he'd want to live back at home, since that's where his businesses are. I shift in my seat a little, excited to talk about what his plans are and what he wants to do while he's here, but as I do, he gets up and says he needs to go to the bathroom.

I WATCH his back as he walks away and then my eyes drift to the other side of the booth. He left his wallet and phone on the table. My fingers itch to grab it. I need to know who's been calling him. It's not that I don't trust him, I know that he's not up to anything, but I just need to know what he's avoiding. I have a good guess it's Tony. Sandra's been messaging me a lot about it, about the two of them not getting along. Derek told me not to tell her the truth though. He doesn't want anyone to know what happened between them.

But it fucking kills me. He already lost his mom. I don't want him losing his best friend too.

His phone goes off again.

I can't resist anymore.

The very thought that it could be Tony makes me need to look. This isn't a habit that I'm going to be making. I'm not gonna be going through his things. Right now I'm just gonna blame it on curiosity. I'm quick to yank it off the table and hit the little button on the side. I scroll down: fifteen unread texts, five missed calls, and two voicemails.

All from Tony.

I hit the button on the side of the phone again and the screen goes black as I slide it back in its place. Right where he had it. It hurts to see how their friendship has deteriorated. I don't know what to think about Tony. I know my sister loves him. And from what Derek says, Tony really did love Derek's mom. I don't know if I could've done what he did, but I know she was ready to go. She had some good moments in her life. She had some bad moments, too. She was ready for all of it to be over though. I know that's true. So does Derek. Deep down in there somewhere. He knows. Even if it hurts.

I wonder if things will ever go back to how they used to be between Tony and Derek. I hope so, since it doesn't look like Tony's going to be leaving Sandra's side anytime soon. My throat dries, and I take another sip of water as Derek slides back into his seat.

"Sandra was asking when we were going to be back in

town again," I say softly as he gets comfortable. He stiffens slightly.

"Is he gonna be there?" He asked, his voice hard.

"You know he is, Derek," I answer him. My finger brushes along the cold side of the glass as I wait for him to respond.

He clenches his jaw and looks outside of the window to his right. "She was ready," I dare to speak and try to convince him. "You told me yourself, you didn't realize it until after everything happened, but she was telling you goodbye." It's hard to get out the words, but it breaks my heart to see him and Tony ruined over this. I know in my heart that Tony was only trying to give Derek's mom peace.

Derek's silent. I know he wants to get over this. I know he misses his friend. But right now all he has is sadness and anger. It's something that's just going to take time.

"Are you going to be okay?" I ask him. He looks down at his phone and back up to me. There's a look on his face that lets me know he knows I was snooping. I'm fine with that though. I would've told him anyway. I can't keep any secrets from him.

He's quiet for a minute before taking a deep breath. "I don't know," he admits.

"I'm here for you. No matter what," I tell him as I grab his hand.

"I don't deserve you," he says quietly.

"Yes. You. Do." I emphasize each word.

He doesn't answer me. I don't want him to continue going down this dark path.

Derek cups my face, and looks me in the eye. "I love you, Emma." My heart swells in my chest. I already knew he did. But hearing him say it and knowing he's admitted it to himself makes all the difference.

"I love you too, Derek."

EPILOGUE

Derek
Nine months later

I STARE at the thin cardboard box on the kitchen counter. Inside is a beautiful cake. It's pink with a fondant bow. It's for Sandra. Technically, it's for a little girl, Emma's soon-to-be niece.

They're coming over today, and I'm preparing myself. Every time they come over it gets easier and easier to fall back into the solid friendship I had with Tony before. But there's still a part of me that hates him.

I fucking loved him. He was my brother in every way that mattered. I'm trying to come to terms with everything still.

I know Ma was ready. I know she wanted it. In some ways, I know it was best. But I'd be lying if I said I fully forgive him. Not yet at least. But when we're together, it's getting easier to forget.

"Derek." I hear Emma's soft voice as her small hand touches my arm.

I take in a long breath to calm myself and forget the past before pulling her into my arms. She lets me hold her. It's all I need sometimes. Especially on the hard days.

She pulls away from me and looks into my eyes. "You gonna be alright?" she asks me.

"Yeah, I'll get through it," I tell her honestly. I'm ready to be a happy fucking family. I'm trying at least. Emma needs this. And for her, I would do anything.

Emma told me they're naming her after Ma. It makes me…emotional. In a good way. In the best of ways, I guess. I hope Emma and I have a baby girl one day. I know I won't be able to name her after Ma. So knowing that Tony is going to use her name makes me happy. It makes me really happy, honestly. I haven't told him that yet though.

And they're naming me godfather. Tony seems to think that one day, things will be back to the way they were. He said we're family, and we'll always be family. The last time I saw him, it was almost like normal. It's fucked up in some ways. I feel like I should never forget. As if I should never forgive him. But deep down I know she was ready to go, and at least he had the balls to do what was right and help her go peacefully. I was the selfish one. I know that now.

I know it's true, but some days I don't want it to be true. I want him to take it back. I want my Ma to be here. But in reality she would have passed by now. The only difference is that she would have suffered more.

"It's gonna be alright," Emma says softly.

She pats my chest, and the sparkle from her engagement ring catches my eye. No matter what, he's gonna be in my life, and a part of my family. Tony's knocked up her sister, and I'm marrying Emma. So there's no way of getting around it. I had the inside of her band engraved to read, *Smile today without fear of tomorrow*. Just like Ma always said. They're words I want us to try and live by from now on.

"I promise you." Her hazel eyes plead with me to accept it. And I'm trying. I really am.

"Have I told you how much I love this kitchen?" she says not-so-subtly, to change the subject. I rest my forehead against hers, and give her another small kiss. One day, we will be alright, and things will be like they used to. But for now, I just need to grieve in my own way. And that means getting lost in my sweetheart's touch.

We've been here for a few months now. Ever since she graduated. It's close to downtown, which is where my restaurants are, and close to Emma's new job. She doesn't have to work. I'm only bringing in income from the legit businesses now that I quit dealing, but it's more than enough.

She wants to work though. At least for now she does. Until I put a baby in her.

"You gonna take off next week like I asked?" I ask her.

"Yes," she answers with a bit of skepticism in her voice. She's always bringing home work.

We're taking time off to visit the venue for the wedding. It's a destination wedding, and I'm planning on taking advantage and making this a nice little vacation.

She keeps pushing back the date, and I know it's because of Tony and me. I always pictured him by my side as my best man if I ever got married. And once things are better between us, I know he'll be there for me.

She hugs me tight, taking my mind off of the things that keep me in the past, and reminding me of our future. I kiss her hair. I just need this. Just her. And I'll be alright.

"I love you, Derek," she whispers. I know she does. And I sure as fuck love her.

"I love you too, sweetheart."

ABOUT WILLOW

Thank you for reading Burned Promises. I hope you loved reading it as much as I loved writing it.

If you'd like to read more about the world Derek and Emma live in, read a sneak peek of Dirty Dom in the next few pages.

More by Willow Winters

https://www.willowwinterswrites.com/books/

Stalk me everywhere!

WillowWintersWrites.com
BadBoys@WillowWintersWrites.com

CHECK OUT MY DEBUT ROMANCE

If you haven't already read the first book in the Valetti Crime family series, Dirty Dom (Available Now!), have a little sneak peek:

Dirty Dom

A Bad Boy Mafia Romance
(Valetti Crime Family)

Winter Willows

BLURB

Dominic Valetti is only interested in two things: getting paid and getting laid.

He's a bookie for the Valetti crime family, and he knows his sh*t.

Dom's busy doing business, no time to dabble in social niceties. The women that chase after him wanting more than a dirty, hard f*ck are only gonna get their hearts broken.

That is, until Becca stumbles into his office to pay off her ex's debt. A hot brunette who's just as guarded as he is and has a body made for sin… and for him.

They're not meant to be together. A woman like her

BLURB

shouldn't be with a man like him. He's mobbed up; she's a good girl who deserves better.

When they push their boundaries and cave to temptation, they both forget about the danger. And that's a mistake a man like Dom can't afford.

Will Dirty Dom risk it all to keep Becca safe, or will he live up to his name?

This is a standalone, full-length mafia romance with a filthy-mouthed, possessive bad boy. Guaranteed HEA.

PROLOGUE

Dom
Becca

Dom

I crack my knuckles and stretch out my arms while looking out over the football stadium from my suite. I fucking love that this is my office. But then again, when you do what I do, your "office" can be anywhere. I snatch my scotch from the bar and tell Johnny to grab our lunch. Taking a seat on the sectional, I grab my phone to look at my schedule. My first drop off should be here soon.

Becca

I'm so fucking nervous. I click my phone on and see I have fifteen minutes to find the bookie's suite. I grab my purse tighter, holding the Coach Hobo closer to my side. I've got 12k in cash under a scarf and the idea that I'm going to be mugged and then killed by the bookie is making my blood rush with adrenaline and anxiety. I can't believe Rick would put me in this position. Shit. I'm such a bitch. I swallow the lump in my throat and square my shoulders to keep the tears pricking the back of my eyes from surfacing. Now is not the time to think about Rick. And it's not like he asked me to do this. His problems keep coming after me and I wanted to cover my bases.

THE KNOCK at the door seems hesitant and that makes a deep, rough chuckle rumble in my hard chest. Whoever's behind it is scared and I live for that fear. They're right to be scared. I didn't get where I am today by being kind and understanding. Fuck that. I'm a ruthless prick and I know it. My chest hollows for a fraction of a second, but I shut that shit down ASAP. I'm a tough fucker and I'm not going to let some pussy emotions make me weak. Some days I wish I didn't have to be such a cruel asshole. I don't like fucking guys up, breaking their legs and hands or whatever body part they pick – if I let them choose. But they know what they're signing up for when they do business with me. Damn shame they don't have a doctorate degree in statistics from Stanford, like me. A devilish grin pulls at my lips. If you're gonna be making bets with me, you better be ready to pay up.

I wipe the cold sweat from my hands and onto my skirt, ball my small fist tighter and knock on the door a little harder. I wonder if the people walking by know why I'm here. I swallow thickly, feeling like a dirty criminal. My eyes dart to an older woman with kind eyes and grey-speckled hair pushing a caterer's cart. I'm sure she knows. I'm sure everyone who looks at me knows I'm up to no good.

My eyes glance from left to right as I wait impatiently. Sarah's waiting outside and I have to pick up my son from soccer practice soon. I lick my lower lip as the nerves creep up. I'll just pretend this isn't real. Just hand them the money and walk away. Back to real life. Back to my assistant and move on with my normal, non-threatening, everyday life.

I TAKE my time getting to the door. No matter how much money they owe me, or how much they've won, they need to know that I do everything whenever the fuck I please. If they have to wait, they have to wait. But I sure as shit don't wait for them. I open the door and my cold, hard heart pumps with hot blood and desire.

A petite woman in fuck-me pink heels and a grey dress that clings to her curves and ends just above her knees is staring back at me with wide, frightened hazel eyes. Her breasts rise and fall, peeking out of the modest neckline. Her black cardigan is covering up too much of her chest and I barely resist the urge to push it off her shoulders. My eyes travel along her body in obvious appreciation before stopping at her purse. She's clinging to it like it's her life line. My jaw ticks, what's a woman like her doing making bets with a guy like me? Johnny handles most of that shit now. We aren't supposed to take bets from women. I don't like it. I'm definitely going to have to ask him about her.

The door opens and I nervously peek up at the gorgeous man looking down at me through my dark, thick lashes. The lines around his eyes means he's every bit the man he looks, but his devilish white-toothed grin gives him a boyish charm meant to fool women like me. He's fucking hot in a black three-piece suit that's obviously tailored to fit his large chiseled frame perfectly. With that crisp, white button-down shirt and simple black tie you'd think he was a young CEO, but his muscular body, piercing blue eyes and messy brunet hair that's long enough to grab, makes him a sex god. Lust and power radiate from his broad chest as his eyes travel down my body. He looks like a man who knows how to destroy you.

A wave of desire shoots through me when my eyes meet his heated stare. My breathing hitches and I swallow down my distress with my treacherous body. I'll just give him the money Rick owed him and get the fuck out of here. At the reminder of why I'm standing in his doorway, I push my purse towards him.

I GRIN at her obvious nervousness and cock a brow, "Purses aren't my style, doll." Pulling the door open wider, I step aside, just enough for her to get through. Her soft body gently brushes mine as she walks through the small opening I gave her. The subtle touch sends a throbbing need to my dick and I feel it harden, pushing against my zipper. She hustles a little quicker when I lean closer to her. Her hips sway and I stifle a groan when I see that dress clinging to her lush ass. Fuck, I want that ass. I never mix business with pleasure, but there's an exception to every rule. Something about her just pulls me in. Something about the way she's carrying herself. Like she needs me, or I need her. My dick jumps as she turns around to fully face me. Fuck, at least one part of me desperately wants her attention.

His body touching mine makes every nerve ending in my core ignite; I nervously squeeze the strap of my purse. I just want to get the hell out of here. My stupid heart is longing for comfort. My trembling body is aching with need. What the hell is wrong with me? It's only been three days; I should have more respect for Rick than this. I will the tears to go away. I just want to be held. But I know better. This man staring back at me, he isn't a man who will hold me. I take in a gasp of air and turn around to face the man my husband owed money to while digging in my purse to gather the bundles of cash.

"Is it all there?" **I have no fucking clue who she is or what she's supposed to be giving me. Johnny has the list, but he's not back yet with our lunch. It's a rarity that I even have to speak during drops. I just like to watch. And when it comes to people not paying up, it's best that I'm here.**

"I'm sorry it's late." His rough fingers brush mine as I hold out the thick bundle of hundreds. His touch sends a shot of lust to my heated core and I close my eyes, denying the desperate need burning inside me. It would feel so good to let him take me the way a man should. I haven't been touched in months. I haven't felt desire in nearly a year, and I know for a fact, I've never felt such a strong pull to a man, never wanted to give myself to someone like I do him.

"What about the interest?" **Her eyes widen with fear and her breath stalls as her plump lips part. If it's late, then she should know to pay that extra 5% per day. Compounded. Johnny should've told her all that shit. But judging by her silence and that scared look on her face, she doesn't have a clue. A grin pulls to my lips, but I stifle it. I want her to think I'm mad. I want her to feel like she owes me. I don't want her money though. She can pay me in a way I've never been paid before. I don't accept ass as payment, but for her, fuck yeah I'll take it.**

The man on the phone said not to worry about being late. He said he was sorry for my loss and that he understood. I feel my breath coming up short as a lump grows in my throat. Fuck! What the hell am I going to do? Fucking Rick, leaving me with this shit to deal with. I wish I could just fucking hide as these damn tears start pricking my eyes. My hands start to shake as I realize I'm trapped in the bookie's suite and I owe him money.

"Aw, doll. Don't cry. We can work something out." Her bottom lip's trembling and her gorgeous hazel eyes are brimming with tears. I feel like a fucking asshole for taking advantage of the situation. But then again, what the fuck did she expect? First, she made a bet with a bookie – not fucking smart on her part. Then she comes late to hand over the dough. She had to know there'd be consequences. She parts her lips to respond, but she's too shaken up. My heart clenches looking at her small frame trembling with worry.

I'll make it good for her. She looks like a girl I could keep. My brows furrow as I reach out to brush her cheek with my hand. I'm not sure where that thought came from, but the more I think about it, the more I like it. She closes her eyes and leans into my touch as I wipe away the tear trailing down her sun-kissed skin. As I reach her lips, I part them with my thumb.

I hate the bastard tears that've escaped. I feel too raw and vulnerable. I can't help but to love the warmth of his skin. How long has it been since someone's touched me with kindness and looked at me with desire? I *need* this. I need to be held. If only for a little while. His thumb brushes my bottom lip and I instantly part them for him. He can hold me for a moment. I can pretend it's more. I can pretend he really wants me. I can pretend he loves me.

BURNED PROMISES

Fuck, she's so damn perfect. Leaning into me like she really wants me. Like she needs me. She radiates sweet innocence, but there's something more about her, something I can't quite put my finger on. A sting of loneliness pulses through me. I was playing with the thought of having her on her knees in exchange for payment. But I want more. I want her to fucking love what I do to her. I'll make her want me when it's over. A coldness sweeps through me. They always want me after, but it's for the money, not for me. A sad smirk plays at my lips as she licks my thumb and massages the underside with her hot tongue. Fuck, I'll take it. If she only wants me for my money, I'll take it. I feel a burning need to keep her.

My brows furrow in anger at my thoughts. My fucking heart is turning me into a little bitch. "Strip. Now." My words come out hard, making her take a hesitant step back as I pull my thumb from her lips. I instantly regret being the fucking asshole I am. But I can't take it back. I turn my back to her, to lock the door. I slip the gun out from under my belt and easily hide it from her sight to set it down on the table by the door. God knows what she'd think if she got a look at it.

My body flinches as the hard sound of the door locking echoes through the room. He moves with power and confidence, his gaze like one of a predator. I swallow my pride and slip off my cardigan. I don't need pride and self-respect right now; I need a man to desire me. The thought and his hungry eyes on me has me peeling off my dress without hesitation. I don't care if this is a payment or if he's just using the interest as an excuse to fuck me; I want this. Or at least I want him.

As I reach behind my back to unhook my bra, he reaches for me, wrapping his strong arms around my body and molding his hard chest to mine. His lips crush against mine and I part them for his hot tongue to taste me. He kisses me with passion and need. His hard dick pushes into my stomach. The feeling makes my pussy heat and clench. Yes. The tears stop, but my chest is still in agony. *Make it go away, please. Take my pain away.*

SHE FUCKING NEEDS ME; I can feel it. And I sure as fuck need her. I don't even hesitate to unleash my rigid cock from my pants. I rip her skimpy lace panties from her body, easily shredding them and tossing them to the floor. I squeeze her ass in my hands, pulling her body to mine. I slam her against the wall, keeping my lips to hers the entire time. My chest pounds; hot blood pumps through me. I need to be inside her. I line my dick up with her hot entrance, rubbing my head through her slick pussy lips.

Fuck she wants me just as I want her. I slam in to the hilt. She breaks our kiss to lean her head back, banging it against the wall and screaming out with pleasure as I fuck recklessly into her tight pussy. My right hand roams her body while my left keeps her pinned to the wall. Her arousal leaks from her hot pussy and down to my thighs.

My legs wrap tightly around him as he ruts into me with a primitive need. My body knows I need his touch, my heart needs his lips and it clenches as he gives them to me. He frantically kisses me as he pounds into me with desperation. The position he has me in ensures he pushes against my throbbing clit with each thrust. I feel my body building, every nerve ending on high alert.

His lips trail my neck and he leaves small bites and open-mouthed kisses along my neck, my shoulder, my collar bone. He licks the dip in my throat before trailing his hot tongue up my neck. I moan my pleasure in the cold air above us. My heart stills and my body trembles as a numbness and heat attack my body at once. "Yes!" I scream out as my pussy pulses around his thick cock. My body convulses against his as heat and pleasure race through my heavy limbs. I feel waves of hot cum soak my aching pussy. My eyes widen as the aftershocks settle. What the fuck did I just do? I need to get out of here.

She's pushing against me like she can't wait to leave and that makes my damn heart drop in my chest. Fine. It's fine. It's not like this was anything more than a payment. I say that over and over while I turn my back on her to grab my pants. I walk across the suite to grab a tissue for her to clean up from the desk, but when I face her, she's already dressed. My blood runs cold with her dismissal of me and what we just shared. It wasn't just some fuck. There was something there. I've never felt like that before. I never felt THAT before. Whatever it is. I fucking want it. And I'm a man who gets what he wants. My conviction settles as I stride back to her. I'll have her again. I'll make sure it happens.

What the fuck have I done? I need to go. I have to go to my son. I want nothing more than for this man to hold me, but I know that's not going to happen. I'm so fucking stupid. I don't even know his name. These feelings in my fucked up chest aren't the same for him. This was just a payment. The thought makes my heart stop and my chest pain, but I brush it aside. I refuse to be any weaker in front of him. I need to be strong for just a moment longer. I try to fix my hair as best as I can without a mirror. I straighten my back and grab my purse as he walks back over to me.

Women like it when I'm an asshole. Don't know why and I

don't care, but it always has them coming back to me. I definitely want to see this girl again; I fucking need to be inside her as often as I can. So after I walk her sweet ass to the door I give her a cocky smirk and kiss her cheek.

He leans in and whispers against my ear, letting his hot breath tickle my sensitized neck, "Thanks for the payment, doll." With that he turns his back and shuts the door without giving me a second glance. That's the moment the lust-filled hope dies and my heart cracks and crumbles in my hollow chest.

I COUNT the money and start pacing. I need her info from Johnny. I need to know who this woman is. Whoever she is, she's going to end up being mine. Not five minutes after she's gone, Johnny comes back. "The first drop just left. She came with everything, but the interest." I pocket her panties so he won't see them. "Twelve grand right?"

"We didn't charge her interest; she didn't know about her husband's debt until yesterday."

"Since when is that how we do business?" I don't even try to keep my voice down. Blood starts pounding in my ears. "Why the fuck is she paying her husband's debt? He doesn't have the balls to come here himself? He sends his woman!" The words jump from my lips before I have a moment to think.

I'm usually more controlled, more thoughtful. If this job has taught me anything it's that silence is deadly and being a hot head will get you killed. But I'm shaking with rage. Anger seeps out of my pores. Anger that she's married to a fucking coward and a bastard. But more than that, I'm fucking pissed that she's taken.

Johnny shakes his head in confusion and slows his

movements as he takes in my rage. "No it's not like that. He died last week, heart attack or something."

The moment Sarah sees me, the last bit of my hardened exterior cracks. I feel my lips tremble and bite down to prevent the tears. "What did you do, Becca?" Sarah's pleading eyes makes me feel even shittier. She knows, she can tell. I'm sure I look like I just got fucked. My neck is pulsing from where he was biting me.

Her eyes want me to tell her she's wrong, they're begging me to tell her she's mistaken, but I can't lie. I can feel his cum leaking out of me and running down my thigh. Evidence of my weakness and my betrayal. The tears well in my eyes and I can't stop a few from leaving angry, hot trails down my cheeks. All I can manage to reply is the barest of truths, "I slept with him."

"Don't cry Becca. It's alright."

"Rick just died and I slept with a stranger." I don't keep my own disgust out of my voice.

"It's not like you two were even together in the end anyway. You were separated for nearly two months." My breath comes in spasms as I rest my head on the door of my car. I loved my husband, but I can't remember the last time he held me, the last time we made love. A criminal who probably would've hurt me had I shown up empty handed gave me more compassion and desire than Rick has in years.

MY BREATH CATCHES in my throat. I took advantage of her in a moment of weakness, but I didn't fucking know how vulnerable she was. I slam my fist against the window. I didn't fucking know! A sick, twisted churning makes me want to heave. Fuck, I treated her like some random slut. She probably thinks I'm a fucking animal for doing that to her. Fuck! I knew she needed me. I fucking knew it.

I just needed to be held and feel like I was loved. This shattering in my chest, jagged pieces of glass digging into my heart, it wasn't worth it. It hurts too much. The worst part is that a very large part of me wants, no needs, to crawl back to him and beg him to hold me again. Just one more time.

I wish I hadn't let her go.

I wish I'd never had to meet with him.

I clench my teeth and close my eyes, wondering if I'll ever see her again.

I breathe deep and steady myself to drive away, knowing I'll never see him again.

I hate myself.

I hate myself.

I'm such a dirty bastard.

Dirty Dom, the first in the Valetti Crime Family Series, is Available Now!

Made in the USA
Middletown, DE
07 January 2024